DIRTY
LAUNDRY

Cori Nevruz

5310
publishing

Praise

"A fast-paced, quick-witted, thought-provoking, psychological thriller with incredibly suspenseful and exhilarative turns that **will keep you guessing all the way to the end**. Read it in one sitting. **Couldn't put it down!**"

— Review by David Rountree, Award-Winning Director

"**Had me on the edge of my seat.** I devoured this clever and captivating book in one sitting."

— Ana C. Sales, best-selling author

"**Fast-paced and compelling**, Nevruz's story builds and builds, culminating in a tense ending that feels inevitable yet surprising. Her characters and family dynamics are **relatable and believable. An entertaining, engrossing read!**"

— Starred Review

"Amazing novel ... The suspense kept building up throughout the book, **full of plot twists by the end**, which made me breathless. **Definitely recommend.**"

— Starred Review

"Wow! **A tale so realistic it's frightening!** It's slow to build up and then hits you hard. **Outstanding!**"

— Sara Bushway, author of *Honey Beaumont*

"Riveting! It sunk its teeth in and **had me recommending it to friends in the first few chapters** and kept me hanging on to see what was going to happen next while slowly pulling me deeper into the minds and lifestyles of the characters."

— Darren Finney, author of *Faithfully Addicted*

DIRTY
LAUNDRY

Not everything is what it seems.

CORI NEVRUZ

Published by

5310 Publishing Company

5310publishing.com

Our books may be purchased in bulk for promotional, educational, or business use. Please contact your local bookseller or 5310 Publishing at sales@5310publishing.com.

ISBN (paperback): 978-1-7771517-9-9

ISBN (ebook): 978-1-7771518-0-5

Author: Cori Nevruz

Editor: Eric Williams, Alex Williams

Cover design: 5310 Publishing

First edition (this edition) released in July 2021.

Also published as *Os Segredos de Samantha* in Brazil and Portugal.

For Bob

Prologue

Police cars, fire trucks, and an ambulance blocked the otherwise quiet, well-manicured boulevard in one of the most desirable family neighborhoods in the quaint town of Masonboro. Likely more curious than concerned, neighbors lined the streets after waking to the sirens and bright flashing bulbs in the dim light of early dawn. Officers were stationed around the large, storybook, suburban home, keeping nosy onlookers at bay. Hushed voices could be heard in the distance, only speculating the cause of the commotion.

"Do you think she had enough?"

"Is he capable of taking things this far?"

"I certainly hope the kids are alright."

"Did she seem unhappy to you?"

While the crowds' size spread as fast as the rumors, a body, lying in a pool of blood, was growing cold on the once inviting front porch.

Chapter One

Though fortune-tellers and superlatives would have us believe otherwise, one's current position in life does not guarantee one's path in the future. The boy who was voted "Most Likely to Succeed" in high school could end up penniless on the street, and the kid who dropped out of school could make millions on an invention he created in his garage. Some say "old habits die hard," but our behavior and personality are always in a constant state of change. A well-prepared planner could learn to live in a disorganized mess, just as a competitive athlete can learn to lose. However, like people and personalities, not all habits are bad, nor should they be forgotten.

Samantha was always the most driven of her friends. They would tease her for rising early to jog before class or work but freely admitted they were all envious. Only ten years later, those friends would no longer recognize her. Samantha, now an overweight mom of two, would wake just long enough to get her kids off to school before climbing back into bed to binge-watch movies on her tablet while chomping on chips. The woman who was known to keep the most uniquely clean dorm room now placed a dirty bowl in the sink and considered the kitchen clean. She, who was once voted "Most Likely to Rule the World," now suffered from chronic depression under her controlling husband's constant pressure.

Samantha Sullivan was often described with OCD, or as her husband not-so-fondly refers to her, anal-retentive. She is of average height for a woman, with shoulder-length dirty blond hair. She grew up participating in competitive sports and played soccer, on a full scholarship, in college. When there was no one around to challenge her, she would compete with herself. She clung to her schedule like the world would stop spinning without it. She was always at least ten minutes early everywhere she went, and even earlier, when she had someone to meet. That was the proud and confident Samantha that Roger had married.

Roger Sullivan is the high-powered CIO for a Fortune 100 company. He makes great money and works a lot of hours. He travels periodically, but even when he is in town, he is at the office much later than the normal nine to fiver. Roger is 5'10 with the build of a long-distance runner, lean and toned. He has closely-cropped brown hair and is always clean shaved. After dealing with stress all day at his high-pressured job, he hopes that things will be perfect when he comes home. He wants the garage door closed with all yard tools clean and organized perfectly, the house to be spotless, his dinner to be delicious, healthy, and ready to be served to him by his fit, beautiful wife. If anything is off, the night is ruined. If Samantha feels less than her best and greets him in leggings or, God forbid, pajamas, he notices. If, when he pulls in the driveway, the garage was left open from when Samantha went out earlier in the day, or a rake is hung back up with a stray leaf, he notices. If Samantha had a rough day and had to order pizza to be delivered, he notices. He doesn't just notice; he makes sure she knows he notices in hopes that lessons will be learned and the action not repeated. He had to deal with enough issues and incompetence at work, and he did not want to do it at home.

When they were first married, Samantha quickly became aware that even though Roger had eaten take-out or frozen dinners for the previous four years while he was single, he had very high expectations for his wife. She had always been driven and worked very hard. She maintained a perfect GPA in high school while participating in school athletics and clubs to get into a good college. In college, she studied whenever she was not volunteering at the local food bank or working for the Dean part-time. She was one of the first in her area of study to gain employment early fall as a college senior at an exceptional company. She never worked the typical eight-hour workday either but would stay until her work was complete and perfect. It was more than a job to her, it was her career, and she needed to excel.

When she started dating Roger, the idea of being a provided for Stepford Wife sounded like a nice break. How much fun would it be to exercise every morning, shower leisurely, get dressed up, go shopping, make a nice dinner and do whatever was necessary to make sure her husband was happy and relaxed? After working so hard for random bosses, the idea of working hard for the man she loved sounded like a dream.

Samantha and Roger's courtship had been a whirlwind. Roger always bragged about his unflappable talent for judging character on sight. Only months into their relationship, he told Samantha that she was the one for him and that he was ready to get on with their life together. Why wait? He was never wrong about people.

They had their first big argument as a married couple over the temperature at which they set their thermostat in their house. The argument topic didn't even matter after the first few minutes when all of Roger's words became hurtful. Samantha was so shocked by his anger that she couldn't even defend herself or fight back. When she was growing up, her family had an unspoken rule... you could argue, and you could fight, but there were some things you could never say to the people you loved. Tell me that I am wrong, but don't make things personal and about things that I cannot change.

She was hurt and would never forget the horrible things Roger said to her. She wanted him to apologize. She ached for him to let her know that even though he said terrible things, he loved her and certainly never meant it. She tried one time to broach the subject, in hopes of allowing him to talk about his outburst, but she could still see the anger burning in his eyes through her soul. But as weeks of silent treatment followed and though she would never erase those hurtful words from her mind, she began to feel like she did something wrong, like she needed to apologize. Her skin on her fingers was picked raw down to the first knuckle, and she wondered if this was how she punished herself. The physical pain, however, did nothing to lessen the agony of her unbearable silent torment.

One Friday afternoon, Roger snapped out of his anger, so things seemed back to normal. She did not want to bring up their argument, but she really wanted to talk about his reaction so they could work through it together. They met less than six months ago and have only been married for two. Unlike couples who spend years getting to know each other, they needed to work harder to understand each other and make their marriage work. When Roger was in a good mood later that evening, she asked him if he thought things were okay between them.

"One thing you will learn about me is that I do not fail. I do not make bad choices. I know people. When I said that you are the one for me, I meant it. Not only will I never be wrong, nor will I ever make a mistake, but I truly believe that knowing people is my gift. I will never leave you, and you will never leave me."

At that time, after weeks of feeling abandoned, undeserving, and inexplicably guilty, that was exactly what she wanted, what she needed to hear. Clearer heads may have taken Roger's statement as a warning, but all she wanted at that moment was his love and commitment. She ran to him and held him tight until he picked her up and carried her off to the bedroom where they spent the rest of the weekend.

Chapter Two

A month later, Samantha was pregnant with their first child, just three months since they were married. Being nauseated twenty-four hours a day, seven days a week, for nine whole months made her new role as a perfect wife nearly unattainable. No one wants to get dressed up when they are hovering over the toilet for most of the day. She couldn't even look at raw meat or any dairy product without getting sick, making cooking a challenge. And she certainly didn't feel sexy with her rapidly-growing body.

Roger was excited about the pregnancy but definitely did not want things to change. He may have been more excited that he was continuing his bloodline, or maybe even having a son to carry on the Sullivan name than he was to be actually having a child. He made sure to point out when any weight was gained in Samantha's hips, legs, or really anywhere but her belly. He criticized Samantha's cooking daily as well as her lack of dedication to her fitness routine. His temper seemed to get worse, or maybe it was just his fuse that seemed shorter. He was quick to assign blame even when there was a blameless event. Once, when he came home from work, he tripped over a slightly raised brick as he walked across the patio. "What the heck, Samantha?" he yelled. Heck was about as bad of a word as he would use around her, but his voice and face told her immediately that his anger was at a much higher level than 'heck.' Samantha laughed, wondering how that could have possibly been her fault. In fact, it was no one's fault, really, unless he wanted to yell at the brick. It seemed so silly yet, after getting the cold shoulder from him again for the following two weeks, she realized it was a bigger deal than she originally thought. Eventually, she became overwhelmed with guilt and the need to apologize like she did something wrong, maybe by not noticing the brick was raised and maybe even repairing it. One day, he walked up the front stairs to the house from his car when his jacket caught on a nail protruding from the wooden railing. "What the heck, Samantha?" he screamed so loud, she was afraid neighbors would hear. This time, rather than laughing, she ran to help him get his jacket off the nail, apologized, and told him she would mend the tear, though small and almost undetectable, right away.

Pregnancies can be tough on more than just the mom. The anticipation can be exciting but also exhausting, not to mention the hormonal rollercoaster of emotions. But people tend to glance over what the dad goes through. Most dads want to be a part of the process but feel so removed since it does not happen to their bodies. Roger was clearly excited about the pregnancy but lacked understanding of what Samantha was going through. He was envious of her immediate connection with the baby she was carrying and was spiteful when she complained of feeling sick or sad. He also had the continuing burden to financially support his growing family. His company happened to be merging with another during the pregnancy. Ten of the thirteen executives that were part of his original company had already been sent packing as the new company took over. Fortunately, Roger was still employed but had little confidence that the position was his for long. Roger helped build the company and was directly responsible for making it profitable and sellable. Now he had to prove himself all over again to a new Board of Directors. He dared not share too much information with Samantha. He did not want to upset her or add unnecessary stress to their baby. Carrying around the additional tension with no one to vent to or confide, put him very on edge as much as he tried to hide it.

Once Roger, Jr. was born, Roger seemed to let go of some tension and anger. He was not just excited to have his very own "Mini-Me," but was looking forward to things getting back to normal. Things like the meals, Samantha's body, and of course, the sex.

On the other hand, Samantha never seemed to be able to put back the pieces of herself. Without question, she loved Junior but was either sad all the time or was very nervous that she was doing something wrong. After the first couple weeks of having the grandparents help, she was finally all alone with Junior.

"Okay, Junior. It's just you and me." she said as she laid her beautiful, innocent little baby in his crib. She walked around the room admiring the nursery. The walls were a beautiful, deep tan. The room was accessorized with light brown and baby blue polka dots. The sheer window coverings were simple yet glamorous, but Samantha debated with herself about whether room darkening shades would've been a better choice for a baby's room. A noise machine playing the soothing sound of ocean waves played on repeat in the background. The changing station was organized just the way she liked it. Her mother had restocked the diapers and burp cloths just before she left. She knew how Samantha was calmed by tidy surroundings. Junior stared up in her direction. The thought of having to keep this little human alive was paralyzing. She stared back at him, concerned. She learned from the doctor that even though it 'looked' like he was looking at her, he couldn't see that far away yet. He looked as though he was ready to smile or maybe even just lie there peacefully, but then he started to squirm and whimper. It only took seconds for that small little whimper to escalate into a full-blown cry. She knew he wasn't hungry; he just ate. She knew he wasn't gassy; he just burped. She knew he wasn't tired; he had been up for only forty minutes or so.

It was her first day solo, and she was already overwhelmed with the pressure that maybe she couldn't handle it. In her eyes, Samantha was already failing at her new job as a mother, by far, the most important job she's ever had.

Her breathing sped up. Her chest was getting warmer and warmer, tighter and tighter. Her head was aching as time was speeding up. Everything around her was moving so fast. She couldn't decipher whether she was going to black out, was seeing spots, or if that was just the wall decoration.

She couldn't call Roger on her first day alone. He would not be happy about the disturbance, plus she couldn't let him know that she was struggling. She couldn't call her parents or in-laws. They would just come back, and that is really not what she wanted either. Was she panicking or was she having a heart attack? The edges of her vision were growing darker and dimmer.

She left Junior in his crib and called 911. "Emergency Services, what is your emergency?" The voice was soothing, considering the work this person did. She sounded like a grandmother who would tell you stories while brushing your hair.

"I'm home with my newborn baby. I am having trouble breathing. My chest hurts. My heart is beating so fast. Actually, I feel like everything is going fast. What is happening to me?"

"Ma'am, it sounds like you are having a panic attack. We will send someone out to your address immediately, but in the meantime, I will be connecting you with a therapist to talk to." the kind voice said.

Almost immediately, another voice came on the line. "Mrs. Sullivan? My name is Monique Daniels." Her voice was just as calming as the first woman. She sounded much younger but with such a beautiful, smooth, relaxing tone. "I hear you have a newborn at home. Congratulations. Is it a boy or a girl?"

Confused about the line of questioning, she quietly answered "Boy."

"Oh, little boys love their mamas! What a wonderful blessing. What is his name?"

"Uh, his name is Roger. He is named after my husband. We call him Junior."

"Wonderful. Is Junior with you right now?" she asked as if she was asking if it was raining outside.

"Yes. Well, no. He is in the crib in his room. I am in my bedroom."

"Great. Is Junior awake right now?"

"Yes, crying." Samantha muttered with shame in her voice.

"If he is in his crib, he is totally fine. Close the door, turn off the baby monitor. He will be fine. Right now, we need to talk about you. Okay?" She paused, then continued. "Start by taking deep breaths. Inhale, hold it, count to four, exhale, count to four, and repeat. Try that for me, please."

Samantha was already slightly less panicked since she started talking to Monique. She took a few deep breaths in and out and listened to the relaxing sounds of ocean waves through the wall from Junior's room. Her vision became less clouded and her chest was not as tight. She began to relax.

"Now, Samantha, please tell me how you are feeling right now."

"A little bit better. I thought I was having a heart attack because my heart was beating so fast, and my chest was so tight, I got frantic. I don't know what to do. I was so completely out of control…"

"Babies do not come with instruction manuals. Those of us who like to be in control are often uncomfortable with situations out of our control. Keep taking your deep breaths, remember that you are okay. Your baby is okay. Once you feel calm, I want you to give your primary care physician a call to get a referral to see a therapist. You are likely dealing with a wide range of emotions that are a difficult yet completely normal part of becoming a mother. Until you can schedule some time to see someone, you can always talk to the therapist on duty here, that's me, or whoever else is working at the time. You are not alone, and it is okay to ask for help."

Monique's words comforted her like a soft, warm blanket. She remembered feeling this way when she was sick as a child. Her mom would feed her saltine crackers and ginger ale, tuck her into her bed, making her feel safe, secure, and cared for. Monique had that same effect.

She had no idea how she would bring this up with Roger but decided this was too important to hide.

Roger, of course, treated her panic attack and possible depression like a flaw. He couldn't understand how someone who sat around the house all day with a baby, a baby that didn't even do anything yet, could be stressed out. Changing diapers, feeding a baby, and even napping when he naps did not compare to his stress. Despite his apprehension and without legitimizing Samantha's stress, he agreed to let her see a therapist, if necessary, to get the medication she needed. However, he seemed to be under the impression that the medication would just 'make her better.' Once she was better, she could just stop taking it, and everything would go back to normal. But as a very private man, Roger did not want her talking to a stranger about their home life. She needed to stick to conversations about whatever these 'baby blues' were and just 'fix it, already.'

Within a week, she began taking medication for depression and started seeing a therapist. Her doctor gave her a list of his recommendations of who she should call for therapy. She started at the top of the list, called everyone, and scheduled with the first person to fit her in for an appointment.

The first doctor that could see her was Dr. Sand. She always envisioned therapy being like it is in old movies. The patient lays on the stylish lounge or fancy leather recliner facing away from the doctor. That would've been easier, not having to look at the person, not having to see their reactions or their attempt to cover their reactions. Instead, she sat on a large couch that was so plush that she sunk into it so deep, she wondered how she would stand when it was time to go. Dr. Sand sat less than five feet in front of her on a tall, hard-backed chair. With his sparse, grey, wiry hair combed over his bald pink head, beady black eyes magnified by his quarter inch thick glasses and crepe-like skin, he personified an evil character from a spy movie. Before they got started, she wanted to figure out what the different types and levels of seating in his office represented, but he picked up his clipboard and pencil, which indicated, to her, the start of their session.

Dr. Sand didn't appear to believe her when she told him that she had a wonderful childhood and had no problems with her parents. He must see a lot of patients with mommy and daddy issues. Samantha would try to explain to him that she was just sad, but not for any reason in particular. Dr. Sand would give her a condescending shake of the head with a "bless-your-heart" look, write down a quick note. Then he would change the subject, asking about the men in the neighborhood where she grew up. Dr. Sand seemed obsessed with the idea that an older man was somehow responsible for Samantha's depression.

Dr. Sand also seemed to believe in the power of the unspoken word. When she came in and sat down, he would just stare at her for what seemed like an eternity until she finally would say something about the weather or some other small-talk subject. After the first few visits, she knew that she was unlikely to continue treatment with Dr. Sand, but she did take one piece of good advice from him. Dr. Sand was big on journaling. He sent her home with the assignment to buy a journal and spend time writing at least once a day. He said, "write anything from a few sentences about your day to a deep dive into her feelings and, specifically, what is happening when those feelings arise.

Samantha set out to visit her local bookstore and picked out a journal. She even made her first journal entry about her selection criteria.

Journal Specifications:
- *Not too big (not letter-sized)*
- *Not too small (not pocket-sized)*
- *Spiral-bound (easier to turn and write on both sides)*
- *Lined (wide-ruled, not college-ruled)*
- *Something inspirational but not cheesy on the cover*

She was scheduled to see Dr. Sand a week later. She was committed to giving it a good try, even though she doubted he would be of any help at all. She journaled every day that week, mostly when she tried to get Junior down for a nap. The entries were bland and boring and were obviously just there to appease Dr. Sand, and he had no problem calling her out at her next appointment.

"Have you ever had an argument with your parents?" he asked.

"I think it is time to lay off the parent questions, to be frank," Samantha said before she knew what was coming out of her mouth.

"I understand your frustrations here; just bear with me. Have you ever had an argument with your parents?" he queried once again.

"Yes, of course.... maybe even a lot as a teenager," she answered.

"Did you ever go to school and complain about your parents, to a friend or boyfriend, after an argument?"

"Oh, yes. Most of what my best friend Suzanne and I talked about were boys, music, and all the things our parents didn't understand about us, or even that they seemed to have forgotten what it was like to be a kid," she confirmed.

"Do you have someone in your life, now, that you can complain to …vent to?" he asked with a smirk.

"I don't have arguments with my parents anymore." She stated, returning the condescending look.

He just stared at her. The silent treatment again... He waited to see if she would catch on, or even to admit that she didn't. After what seemed like ten minutes but was probably more like two, she said, "I don't like to air my dirty laundry. It is not anyone else's business what my private life, or my relationship with my husband, is like."

"So, you don't have an outlet or any way to work through your feelings. I can see if you don't feel comfortable talking about your relationship or family to just anyone, but you need someone to talk to. That person can be me if you are willing to open up. I do not know you or your family personally, and I am not here to judge you, but to be a sounding board to whom you can voice your worries, feelings, and concerns." he explained.

Samantha returned the silent treatment. She just stared at him. She knew he was right. She remembered what a calming release it was to vent to a friend and have them validate her feelings and always take her side. She remembered the giant weight lifted off her chest when she spoke the previously unspoken worries, but she did not like this guy. He was constantly smirking as if he just caught her saying something that he knew she would say. She kept expecting a speech bubble to appear over his head, saying "Everything is going exactly according to my plan."

After a few minutes, Dr. Sand spoke again. "If I cannot be that sounding board for you, maybe your journal can be. Let your journal be your close, non-judgmental, forgetful, fully-supportive friend that won't talk back. Writing those feelings down on paper will help with that weight you've been carrying around. Not to mention, a journal will not gossip about you to others. Your personal thoughts and feelings stay private."

Samantha continued to stare until he added. "But you have to be honest with yourself. You need to write more than just your to-do list. Don't do it for me, do it for you."

Samantha nodded and walked out without making another appointment.

***

Within a couple weeks of her appointment with Dr. Sand, Samantha began to feel better. She was adding a bit more details to her journal, and just when she started to get paranoid that someone would find it, her medication kicked in. She went from feeling on edge all of the time to feeling very laid back. This was a drastic change for someone who had lived their life as a Type A driver. Samantha always wanted control and learned her lesson that she had no control over when Junior would eat, nap, nurse, or how long he would sleep at night. To give her a small feeling of control, she created intricate charts and graphs in her journal to track his eating and sleeping habits. She thought that if she could find a pattern or gain any insight over how he 'worked,' she could regain control over her life. By the time her new medication started working, she was fine with just going with the flow. No schedule, no worries. Who needs a shrink when she can just take medication to fix her flaws?

She continued to journal as her paranoia subsided. She knew Roger had better things to do than snoop through her desk and read her girly journal.

Chapter Three

Samantha packed Junior and some snacks and drinks into the stroller to go for a walk to pass the time. The minutes of every day ticked by slowly. She enjoyed spending time at home with Junior, but he just nursed, cried, and slept. Sure, it was fun to look at his cute little dimpled chin and those chunky legs that looked like they were wrapped in rubber bands. But, staring at a baby for twelve hours a day became tedious. They walked around their small neighborhood, occupied mostly by young couples or retired empty nesters. There were no sidewalks to walk on or other new moms to chat with. The people were kind and would dote on little Junior, but she yearned for someone to compare notes to justify her lack of energy and let her cry for a few minutes. She wanted a confidant on a similar path, a best friend.

It would be nice to live in a place with nice walking trails, a playground, or even benches by a pond where she could sit and journal as Junior fell asleep in his stroller. The idea sounded so peaceful, yet she continued to stumble on the very edge of the road when cars drove by.

An adorable elderly couple she had seen periodically on her walks came into view. They smiled when they saw her and talked amongst themselves until they were close enough to talk with Samantha.

"Good morning, dear." the kind woman said to her. She was accustomed to people only addressing Junior when they would pass, but this woman looked at her like she only cared about her and her well-being.

"Good morning," Samantha replied.

"How are you holding up? I remember when my kids, now grown and married with kids of their own, were little. I had such a hard time." Her husband rolled his eyes, she elbowed him to get him to walk away and continued. "He had no idea because he worked all of the time, but I thought it was very hard to have babies. I loved it when they were older, and I could have conversations with them, I could watch their games and competitions, laugh with them, cry with them, but it was really hard for me when they were babies."

This woman somehow saw right into her heart. Tears began to well up in Samantha's eyes.

"When you have your sleepless nights, exhausting, repetitive days, just remember, every stage in your child's life is better than the last. I remember being devastated at the end of every phase, starting kindergarten, their first girlfriend, going to college, moving out, getting married... but each new chapter of their lives is a new chapter in yours, and it is amazing." She smiled, patted Samantha on the shoulder, jogging to catch up to her husband.

Samantha took a deep breath, realizing she was holding it in, out of fear that with her exhale would come ugly tears. But she didn't cry. The words of that incredible woman would stay with her forever and gave her the hope that she desperately needed.

Chapter Four

Even after what was probably more than a year, and with more medication than should be allowed, Samantha was still trying to dig out of her dark hole of depression that just kept getting deeper and deeper. Nothing got easier. In fact, even her normal everyday tasks seemed to get harder. She was more laid back with the medication but still could hardly keep her head above water.

One morning, Roger walked out of the bedroom, grabbed his briefcase and cell phones then walked into the kitchen where Samantha was waiting patiently. Roger had his quarterly Board of Directors meeting today and was more focused than usual, if that was possible. Knowing this, Samantha stood by the counter in a short, flowery sundress and sassy heels that made her legs look great. She was wearing makeup, but it didn't quite cover the bags under her eyes, or the fresh pimples on her chin. She hoped it would be a good morning even though she was already exhausted from getting up early with Junior.

"Rats nest, today, eh?" Roger said, walking right by her to grab his prepared smoothie and coffee cup as if she wasn't even there. Not a thank you or even an acknowledgment that she had prepared everything for him, kept Junior quiet, and got the kitchen cleaned up before he came in. She looked at her reflection in the microwave and noticed that she forgot to brush or do anything with her hair that chaotic morning.

"Enjoy your 'Life of Reilly'!" he shouted in a patronizing voice as he walked out the door.

She had never heard this idiom before meeting Roger. She remembered when they first met, they would occasionally meet for lunch. They always ended up sitting next to young, seemingly independently wealthy groups. The first time, Roger commented about these rich 'kids' who lived in penthouses bought by daddy, who didn't have to work and could just go to lunch and hang out all day, Living the Life of Reilly. Apparently, originating an old song called "Is That Mr. Reilly, living the life of Reilly means living the easy life, an existence marked by luxury and a carefree attitude. It got to be a joke between them when they would go to lunch. They would pretend to switch places and talk about what they would do after their exhausting morning of going to the spa followed by lunch. It was nice when they used to laugh together. It was nice when they were on the same team. Now, when he told her to enjoy her 'Life of Reilly', he never said it like he really wanted her to enjoy her day. He said it like he hoped she would choke on her blessed life.

<u>Monday:</u>

Not a good start. As far as Roger is concerned, Junior sits in a swing all day while I watch soap operas and eat Bonbons. He has no idea that even with my new chilled out, drugged up self, how exhausting my day can be. It is certainly no Life of Reilly. It may be a rough comparison, but I feel like that old US Army commercial, "WE DO MORE BEFORE 9AM THAN MOST PEOPLE DO ALL DAY," not that I would compare taking care of my baby to fighting terrorists, but still, my first two hours alone were a whirlwind.

Junior woke up with a piercing scream, as usual, at 5:30am. I changed his diaper, fed and burped him, then tried to get a quick shower/get dressed/look presentable for Roger while Junior whines in his playpen. I head to the kitchen and strap Junior into his highchair. The morning is pretty much me trying to find somewhere to securely anchor Junior to prepare myself for Roger. Do I look nice? Is his coffee the right temperature? Is the kitchen clean? Did I put Roger's breakfast smoothie in his favorite cup? Is there dust on the top of the refrigerator... Lord knows, Roger will check...

When I can finally get out of the door, without fail, Junior will fall asleep in the stroller when I am on the farthest point of my walk, and I hurry home to get him to bed, which fails. So, I got to the store, but Junior's meltdown has me leaving a full cart of groceries behind, again.

I feel like I have been up for days, and it is only 8am! My eyes hurt as if I have been crying for hours, I am physically and mentally exhausted, and I feel down in the dumps but not sad. Is this what medicated sadness feels like?
Living the Life of Reilly, my ass.

Chapter Five

Junior, now a toddler, and Samantha set out early to go to the mall to buy a new outdoor gas grill. She kept the interior of their grill very clean, but the outside was getting rusty, so it really disgusted Roger. The mall didn't open until ten in the morning, but Sears opened at nine and had an exterior entrance, so she could get in without walking through the mall. She parked outside in the vacant lot and walked to the back of the car to take out the stroller. Junior is what Samantha likes to call a 'runner.' She has to secure him into his stroller any time they venture out, or he will run away from her, and she didn't like the idea of putting him on a leash like a dog. Her frequent anxiety intensified to the point of almost having a panic attack any time he was out of his stroller. But the mall itself was not open yet, and not too many people were around. She hoped to run in, grab the grill and run out before any crowds showed up. Surely she could let Junior just hold her hand for this quick little errand. She closed the trunk, leaving the stroller behind and walked around to let Junior out of the car.

The two walked hand in hand to the front door. The doors were unlocked, but the store was like a ghost town. Everything was completely silent. There were no voices, beeping of machines, or even music playing. Samantha walked around the corner and saw a few employees in the distance. Before she knew it, Junior shook her hand loose and bolted around the corner to the next aisle. She turned the corner, and to her surprise, no one was there. She listened for a few seconds for his loud footsteps but heard nothing. She stopped and opened every laundry hamper to see if he crawled into one, but Junior was nowhere to be found. She started to panic and ran.

When Samantha reached the end of the aisle, she turned to run past the next group of shelves hoping she would find where Junior had disappeared to. But, just as she took off, she slipped and fell hard on the linoleum floor. She cried out with pain. She screamed with frustration. She yelled in pure fear. She stood back up as fast as she could, pain searing through her hip and elbow, leaving both of her shoes in the spot where she fell. She ran past a "Caution, Wet Floors" sign and screamed at the woman behind the register, "You couldn't have mopped before you opened? I fell flat on my ass and cannot find my son. Call security! Lockdown the store! Someone, please do something! Why are you still standing there?!"

She ran up and down every aisle, looking for any place Junior would think to hide. She called his name sweetly at first, but her voice was growing increasingly panicked.

Samantha heard the door gates close and the screech of a walkie-talkie. She hoped it was a sign that someone was coming to help her rather than stare at her like she was the problem. Samantha slipped again while rounding another corner but grabbed the shelf and caught herself before falling to the floor. Her world was closing in, darkening and becoming blurry around the edges. Her breathing was so rushed she thought she may hyperventilate. A security guard approached her, but she could hardly hear him. Were her ears clogged? She couldn't hear; her vision was fuzzy. What if Junior is not just running around, but someone took him? What would Roger do if she lost their son? How is she going to explain this? She didn't know what was more frightening, losing her son or the backlash of Roger. She shook off the thought and turned away from the security guard to check the door they came in through. She began to worry that Junior had made an escape out to the parking lot or the main part of the mall before they sealed the doors. If he ran, the parking lot is the most dangerous place for him to have gone. As she backtracked through the store, she saw blood droplets all over the floor. She hadn't even noticed that her hand was ripped open between her pointer and middle fingers when she grabbed onto the shelf to keep herself from falling. Just as she was running out the door, she heard in the distance a women's voice yell, "I got him!" She turned and ran as fast as her bare feet would take her towards the disembodied voice.

She was winded when she got to the other side of the store, where Junior jumped on one of the beds. The woman who located him looked at Samantha sympathetically but also with a hint of judgment. Samantha ignored her and ran to Junior and grabbed him in a huge bear hug. Tears fell fast down her face like an open faucet. She was happy, relieved, and thankful to have him in her arms again. She finally snapped out of her public breakdown when she noticed the foul smell escaping Junior's diaper.

Samantha stopped crying, abruptly picked up Junior, and walked straight out of the store to her car. She left Sears that day with no grill, no shoes, leaving blood drippings all over the floor, and a poop stain on a mattress.

Chapter Six

After a week of feeling like her downward spiral had picked up speed, Samantha woke up to feed Junior and ended up with her face in the toilet, gagging. Her stomach lurched and the sour taste of bile coated the inside of her mouth. She chalked it up to getting up too fast, but after losing breakfast, lunch, and dinner into that same toilet, it was obviously more than that. It didn't seem to matter what she ate, or even if she ate at all, she would throw up anyway. She didn't feel feverish or have any symptoms other than feeling severe motion sickness. She took a pregnancy test to confirm her suspicions, and yes, she was pregnant with baby number two.

When they were dating, Samantha and Roger would snuggle on the couch and talk about their hopes and dreams over a bottle of wine. He would prepare gorgeous charcuterie boards for them to snack on and always knew how to pick out the best bottle of wine. He would spoil her by racing to get home before her and making sure everything was clean, the music was thoughtfully selected, and the food and wine would be out and ready for her to enjoy. Roger would talk about his desire to have two kids. No more, because he didn't want to be outnumbered, and no less, because 'only-children were socially awkward.'

Since Junior was born, Samantha was concerned about having more kids. Her mind and body had never recovered, and in her opinion, she was a failure. However, if she didn't give Roger another child, surely she would be to blame, leaving Junior as a socially-awkward, only-child.

So, when she found out she was pregnant, she was thrilled, scared, and relieved all at the same time.

Monday:

Another baby. I wonder if it will be a boy or a girl? Oh my gosh, Roger will be so excited to find out that Junior will not be an only child. It would be fun to have another boy since we have so much boy stuff. But would Roger pick a favorite, and the other would always be left out? What would he treat a girl like? Would she be his princess, or just a girl? Would he let her play sports, or would he want her to stick to cooking and dresses? How am I going to handle two kids when I can barely handle one? I guess I will never go back to work.

Chapter Seven

Samantha paced the kitchen while she waited for Roger to get dressed. They had an appointment with a genetic specialist in less than an hour. Last week, she received a call from her Obstetrician notifying her that the prenatal diagnostic test for Down Syndrome she requested came back positive. Still, the test has a very high rate of false positives, so Samantha and Roger had to make a decision whether to keep the baby or get tested again... She could choose to do nothing, and once the baby is born, find out whether the test was accurate or not.

Samantha had to be prepared. The whole reason why she got tested was to get prepared in case it was positive. She could research Down Syndrome, join support groups, consult experts, and come to terms with what would otherwise be a shock at the baby's birth. The option for her was clear, so she scheduled the additional testing, which included an Amniocentesis. She knew there was a slight risk in this procedure, testing a sample of the amniotic fluid surrounding the baby in the womb. But she also knew that walking around with extremely high-stress levels and fear that she has had since her doctor's call could be very unhealthy for both her and the baby. Her fear was all-encompassing. It kept her up at night, staring at the ceiling with her hand on her belly, just hoping she would feel kicks. Samantha constantly needed reassurance. She was worried about the baby all of the time. The sooner she had an answer, one way or the other, the better.

Roger held her hand as they arrived at their appointment. After the nurse prepped Samantha on the table, she escorted Roger into the room, followed closely by the doctor. The doctor talked them through the entire process and even angled the monitor so she and Roger could both see the ultrasound picture while he was completing the procedure. He explained that the ultrasound was used to help him direct the tube to a place where he can collect the fluid without disturbing the baby, but the parents being able to watch was certainly a bonus he did not want to deprive them of. She watched, shocked, as he pulled out the longest needle she had ever seen. It looked like something that would be used to penetrate elephant skin. The needle was used to insert the tube for collection, but it was still a giant needle that he aimed right at her baby. Samantha's heart rate alert sounded on her watch as she looked over at the nurse, who smiled and calmly told her to relax and close her eyes if necessary. Samantha clamped her eyes shut but could still feel the tears leaking out. She was so scared that something would happen to her baby. She was so scared that she couldn't properly take care of a baby with special needs. She was so scared that Roger would blame any sub-optimal diagnosis on her. She tried not to flinch at the giant stabbing pain.

Roger held her hand a little tighter, and the nurse announced that the tube was inserted. Samantha opened her eyes and looked at the monitor. The baby's head was up rather than down, but the nurse explained that it was still early in the pregnancy and that the baby was likely to move around quite a bit still and could end up head down before delivery. The doctor attached a syringe to the tube, presumably to pull the fluid. As he began pulling the plunger to extract fluid, the baby made a quick movement as if alerted to an intruder. Samantha kept her eyes on the monitor as a tiny, little hand reached out and grabbed the tube, blocking the suction. Samantha laughed and looked up at Roger, who smiled back.

"The suction likely pulled the baby closer to the tube, but it sure looked to me like your baby grabbed my tube." the doctor chuckled. "Now, that is something I have never seen before. Congratulations, your little baby is adventurous." still laughing.

Samantha and Roger stared at each other lovingly as the nurse helped the doctor push the baby away from the tube, so he could complete the fluid pull. They wouldn't have the results for a few days, but the experience made them both more comfortable and at peace with whatever the results would be.

Test Results:

Our baby does NOT have Down Syndrome. The initial blood test was a false positive. The test is faulty, not me. I have felt so guilty that I caused this and that all this is my fault.

I know there will be other problems. He or she will fall and skin their knee, they will fail a test, they will get their heart broken... but they will not have this additional obstacle to overcome. The doctors verified the baby's gender during the exam so we can plan for a big gender reveal. I am so tempted to peak but will try to exercise self-control. When I told Roger about the final test results, he cried. He was so sweet. We embraced, and he rubbed my back. He whispered that he loves me for the first time in ages. Our relief was so powerful, I was sure this would be a turning point in our marriage. But, less than an hour later, he stepped on a Lego that I must have missed when I cleaned up after Junior. I should really be more careful. Everything in my life is so fragile.

Chapter Eight

Roger and Samantha staged a big reveal when they were going to find out if they are having a boy or girl. Samantha wanted to have a big party with friends and family, but Roger wanted it to just be the three (technically four) of them, but they could video it, and she could share with anyone she wanted.

Samantha wore a pink babydoll dress with a big baby blue ribbon over her bump. Junior was wearing blue overalls with a pink gingham shirt. Roger was dressed festively in light blue chinos and a light pink polo. They all stood around a large, refrigerator-sized box with "Boy or Girl" written across the front in bright blue and pink lettering. Samantha picked up Junior and rested him on her left hip as she reached with her right hand to open the box top with Roger. Roger stood on the other side of the box, ready to open with his left hand. He counted them down, "Three, two, one, open!"

They opened the box, and what seemed like hundreds of pink balloons flew into the air. Samantha wanted to celebrate. She was so excited to be having a little girl, but her first reaction was to look to Roger to sneak a peek at his reaction to the news. Roger shouted, "It's a girl!!!" running over and giving Samantha a sweet, gentle kiss, then grabbed a clueless Junior, tossed him in the air, and said, "You're going to have a little sister!"

Roger continued to celebrate while Junior stood in the grass, looking confused as Samantha stopped the video from recording. She wanted to hug Roger and talk to him about all of her plans for decorating for a girl's room, show him the cute Halloween costumes they sell for baby girls, and start talking about names, but Roger turned on his heel and walked inside without a word. The recording stopped, and so did his performance.

Serendipitously, it began to rain. Junior's adorable outfit was getting soaked, but the rain came down at the speed of her tears, starting slow, then becoming a downpour. The rain masked her sadness that came from deep inside her chest. The pain came from deep inside like her ribs; her chest would cave in upon itself. Finally, she took a deep breath, grabbed a drenched Junior, then slowly returned to the house to get them both dried off and cleaned up.

Girl Names:
~~Sierra~~ - *Roger said this sounds too much like a beer*
~~Violet~~ - *Roger said this name reminds him of the floozy on It's a Wonderful Life*

~~Monique~~ *(after the kind therapist on the 911 call) - Roger wondered 'why the hell would we name our baby after someone I talked to once in my life for five minutes'*
Sarah (after Roger's mom)
All of my ideas are being shot down, but the name Sarah is really starting to grow on me. I already love my little Sarah.

***

Everyone told Samantha repeatedly during her pregnancy with Junior that she was sick because she was pregnant with a boy. Her pregnancy with Sarah ended up being just as bad, if not even a bit worse. Not only did she throw up everything she ate, but she also still managed to gain weight. Not just the normal locations like hips, legs, feet, but somehow, her toes, fingers, neck, and nose all seemed to be fatter. She gained fifty pounds during her pregnancy and knew she somehow looked more fat than pregnant. She carried her weight all over.

Friday:
This week's not so helpful and not so encouraging feedback from Roger:
- *Wake up before Junior gets up, so I have time to work out*
- *Take care of chores and cleaning when he naps*

- *Stay up later after Junior goes to bed so I can get everything ready for the next day and not be so rushed*
- *Consider cutting calories back*
- *Maybe I need to change my hand towel every day. Reusing is probably causing my acne breakouts.*
- *Buy some new clothes, so I have something to wear that actually fits my 'new figure' other than yoga pants*
- *Keep Junior up until Roger gets home so he can see his son, but then quickly and quietly get him to bed so he can watch the news in peace*

Chapter Nine

Sarah was scheduled to be born via c-section due to her still being breach. Samantha's parents picked up Junior to take him to their house for a few days, and Roger and Samantha excitedly left for the hospital. It was a beautiful spring morning. The air was warm, but no humidity. The sky was pure blue behind the bright sun, and there was a slight breeze similar to a large palm tree frond slowly waving wind through your hair.

Roger had been quite affectionate during the last few weeks of Samantha's pregnancy. He began to open the door to the car for her the way he used to. He held her hand as they drove down the road. She wasn't allowed to lift a finger at home, and he gave Junior more attention than normal.

The morning was perfect, and Samantha couldn't imagine how anything could go wrong. When they checked in and settled into their delivery suite, Roger paced the room, looking for extra pillows, blankets, or anything to make Samantha more comfortable.

"Is there anything I can get you from the cafeteria?" he asked sweetly.

"No, thank you. I cannot have anything to eat or drink. You can go get something for yourself if you want."

"I don't want to miss a thing," he said, kissing her forehead.

His phone rang. He looked down at the Caller ID, answered it, held up a finger to Samantha, and ducked out into the hallway for a few minutes.

Sarah's Birthday:
Today is the day things change. I can feel it. Sarah will be born today, completing our little family. I feel better today than I have since I was first pregnant with Junior. I will get my life back together. I will get back in shape. I will eat healthily and get back to my pre-Junior weight. Maybe I can even hire a personal trainer. Roger has been so sweet. He has been working so hard for our family. I hope that work is getting a bit less stressful. Now, if I can just pull my weight at home, he will be happy. All I have to do is have a plan. I will work out when the baby naps and maybe even when she goes to bed at night. Junior will be going to preschool a few mornings a week, so maybe I can even get a part-time, work-from-home job. I can see Roger outside my hospital room door on the phone. He doesn't look angry like he normally does on calls. He looks happy. He is smiling. I need to do more of what makes him smile.

The first week that Samantha and Roger were back home from the hospital with Sarah was incredibly peaceful. Junior was back home from Samantha's parent's house, and he was such a good big brother. When she napped, he was quiet, drew her pictures, told her stories, and never argued when Samantha or Roger asked him for help. Sarah slept most of the time. She woke every three hours or so, but she would nurse, burp, and fall right back to sleep. Roger actually took some time off work to take care of household chores and play with Junior, allowing Samantha to nap with Sarah. He cooked amazing meals all week, fresh omelet for breakfast, homemade soup and sandwiches for lunch, and delicious grilled vegetables with seafood for dinner. Samantha would close her eyes to sleep with a satisfied smile, just hoping this feeling would last forever.

The following week, Roger returned to work. Samantha had no trouble making a smoothie and coffee for Roger before leaving for work, with Sarah waking early. She actually wanted to do it. It was not a chore. He had been so wonderful, and she wanted to make him happy. Junior would wake right before Roger left for work, but he was in good spirits. Samantha realized as the day went on how much Roger had helped the previous week. When she was making Junior breakfast, Sarah was fussy and wanted to be held. Samantha's stress level rose exponentially when her kids cried, so she would do whatever was necessary to keep them happy as well. She tried putting the baby in a sling around her front to comfort Sarah and still feed or entertain Junior. When she would cook, she would switch to her backpack carrier, certain that Sarah would catch fire if she cooked over an open flame.

When she would put Sarah down for her nap, not only could Samantha not nap, but Junior wanted to play with her. She found herself using the TV as a babysitter for relief and to get a few minutes of relaxation before Junior would jump up and ask her a question. She was constantly on edge, wondering if his voice was too loud and would wake Sarah. How long would she stay asleep? If she woke up, was it because we are being too loud, or because it is time? How long should she be napping? Her self-doubt increased as the day went on. Was she paying enough attention to Junior? Would he become jealous of Sarah or angry with Samantha?

Roger took some time off his day to call and check in with Samantha and the kids. "How is my family doing?" he said when she answered the phone.

"Fine. Just fine." Samantha started and wondered whether to continue. "It's just that Sarah wants to be held all of the time, so it is really hard for me to get anything done around the house, and Junior wants me to play with him, so I have hardly sat down all day."

"Wow. Sounds like a rough start..." Roger said with sarcasm in his voice. "Let me get this straight... you're complaining about holding a baby and playing with a four-year-old?"

Samantha hoped he was joking. She stayed silent, waiting for the sweet Roger to come back.

"What the heck, Samantha? They're babies. How hard can your day be?"

Chapter Ten

Roger tried to get himself in the proper state of mind to meet with their biggest Enterprise Systems client. He was exhausted. He may not be getting up every other hour to nurse Sarah, but his sleep was still disrupted all the same. Plus, Junior was occasionally awakened as well, and since Samantha was so often with Sarah, Roger had to get up to tend to Junior. It was exhausting to get up in the morning to see what a wreck their house had become over the last several weeks. The laundry was piled up to twice the height of their laundry basket. Dishes were overflowing in the sink with tiny little fruit flies circling them. Roger could smell the overflowing dirty diapers coming from Sarah's room even when he was downstairs. When he opened the refrigerator, he noticed the milk was expired, and there was a drawer full of rotten fruit and vegetables in addition to a few Tupperware containers with unrecognizable, moldy leftovers.

He sighed, grabbed his briefcase as he realized it would be another day of coffee on the go and a vending machine lunch.

There was no reason why Roger couldn't just have his assistant grab him a coffee; she knows exactly how he likes it. He could also have a really nice meal in the company cafeteria where they have a hot bar, a salad bar, and a grill where a chef can cook to your specifications. He had time to go out to lunch or at the very least order food in, but he was so incredibly angry, and he knew by denying himself he would make Samantha feel worse, and that is what he was going for. He wanted her to hear him sigh when he saw the laundry basket or opened the refrigerator. He wanted her to hear him curse under his breath as he opened the towel closet to find that there was nothing clean left. He hoped she noticed his severe handwriting when he added to the grocery list that he had been out of soap for days.

He knew Samantha was tired, but so was he. All she had to do was take care of a toddler and blob baby. He had to manage people, forecast and report quarterly numbers, satisfy customers, and keep costs down. A bad afternoon for her is when Sarah pooped up her back because the diaper didn't hold it all. A bad day for him could mean the loss of his job, livelihood, and security.

He is perfectly aware of all that is riding on his every move. One false step, just one bad decision, and the entire company would shut down, and that is quite a bit more pressure than cleaning shit off a baby's back. Roger often works late in hopes of getting ahead so one day he can take off early and spend some time with the kids. But, the more he works, the more work he seems to have. He has caught Samantha glancing at his phone when he receives a text as if she is concerned that maybe he isn't at work all that time. Maybe she thinks that he is with someone else. It is such a turn off to him how insecure she is, but he does nothing to convince her otherwise. If only she knew that even though the opportunity frequently presented itself, he had no interest at all in other women. Even if he did, he was currently too tired to get aroused.

Chapter Eleven

Samantha sat at the kitchen table, staring at her mess of a home. The dishes were piled high in the sink because she kept forgetting to run the already full dishwasher. She could wash the dishes by hand but forgot to pick up dish soap on her last grocery run. The microwave door was ajar, she could see the splattered marinara sauce all over the walls where she had warmed up leftover spaghetti for Junior and forgot to cover the bowl. The floor was sticky and wet under her feet. She looked down, hoping it was just water but saw it had a slightly yellow tinge. She sighed and tried to remember, hopefully, if they had any Mountain Dew in the house. Junior's highchair was covered in dried up, caked-on food, and a trail of ants were making their way up the legs. A faint alarm sounded, and she jumped up, trying to locate the source. She glanced towards the sounds noticing the freezer was slightly open, and the temperature was getting too high, causing the alarm. She dreaded what she would find when she opened the freezer drawer knowing she made Junior waffles earlier that morning and that it had been hours. She pulled the freezer open and saw that the nearly empty waffle box was jammed in the door, the ice was dripping out of the bottom of the drawer, and the ice cream was completely melted.

She knew the best way for her to tackle her disaster of a home was to make a list. She grabbed her journal and wrote down her list of tasks that needed to be completed. Making a list would remind her of what needed to be done, and even better, she would feel a sense of accomplishment when she checked off each item at the end, appealing to both her love of cleanliness and organization.

Her list was complete and color-coded by the location in the house, accompanied by cute doodles. She stared at it with a smile, pleased by her work. Just as she stood to get started, Junior wandered down the stairs, having just awakened from his nap. She ripped the list out of her journal, balled it up, and threw it in the trash.

Chapter Twelve

Roger returned from work to a quiet house. The kids were likely already in bed since he worked later than usual. The kitchen was cleaner than he had seen in quite a while. He walked through to the living room to set down his briefcase and found Samantha wearing only a t-shirt and what looked to be her old maternity underwear, sprawled out on the couch. She had one leg lifted up against the back of the couch and one on the floor. She was drooling all over the nice pillows and was snoring like a lumberjack. It was not a sexy look, but it took him back to the days when they were dating, and he would spend the night at her house after a late-night out. It brought a slow smile to his face.

He walked back into the kitchen to make something to eat. He opened the refrigerator to find a salad and plate wrapped up for him with a little heart written on the foil. He opened the door to the garbage can to throw out the foil and saw a crumpled-up piece of paper next to the can. He picked it up and saw one of Samantha's lists that she loves so much. It was odd that this was ripped out and not checked off when he knew how much satisfaction the little checkmarks brought her. He threw it in with the foil and carried his plate to the microwave. Roger opened the door to find the inside of the microwave covered in sauce. The microwave could still heat up his food, or he could quickly clean it, but instead, he gagged, threw out his dinner, and ate the cold salad. "What the heck, Samantha?" he mumbled through gritted teeth.

Chapter Thirteen

Samantha awoke every morning, dreading the day in front of her as if her list of tasks was growing hopeless and unbeatable. Samantha was feeling so overwhelmed, as if nothing could ever be conquered. Those large, dark, heavy walls were closing in on her, more and more each day. She needed someone to talk to but knew Roger would just put her down, tell her she was less of a woman because of her depression. She didn't want to reach out to her parents because they would worry. She really would like to get in touch with Dr. Sand again, but she stopped seeing him years ago and knew she would have to start all over with him. She wondered if there was some kind of support hotline she could call. It seemed ridiculous for her to find a new therapist, schedule an appointment, go over all the background and preliminary questions that all therapists start with when in reality, all she needs is someone to chat with on the phone for an hour or even just a few minutes. She guessed this is what most people did with friends and family, but there was so much she wanted to say but didn't want to reveal too much about her personal life. A stranger over the phone would be fine with her. They didn't know her. She wondered briefly if she paid for a phone sex hotline, not knowing if they even existed anymore since the invention of the internet if they would just let her talk.

She had about an hour of quiet in the afternoon when both kids miraculously took a nap at the same time. She searched the internet for message boards that she could read but decided not to register since that was too personal. What if someone got ahold of her login information or somehow identified her? She planned to just read other people's posts for now. She started with the titles:

- *I gained fifty pounds and cannot lose the last five*
- *My husband insists on getting up with the baby at night*
- *My husband took too much time off work, now I am going crazy*
- *My Mother-in-law watches me breastfeed*
- *I am so stressed and don't know who I am anymore*

Samantha didn't feel that she could relate to someone who quickly lost forty-five pounds and complained about the last five. And the two women complaining that her husband is too helpful. She could tell them stories that would make them change their tune. The one about the mother-in-law watching her breastfeed just made her uncomfortable, but the last one looked promising. She clicked through.

I am so stressed and don't know who I am anymore:
My daughter was born three months ago. The birth was straightforward and natural. I didn't gain much weight and have almost lost it all. My husband is very helpful. My daughter is a good girl, sleeps and eats well. Everything is going fine...
But I still do not feel like myself. I no longer feel the way I used to. I love my family but feel so much less happy. I cannot remember the last time I laughed. I am sad. I just feel nothing.
~Jan

She almost closed out of the post after reading the first few lines but stuck with it. If someone who has everything going right for her can feel like this, it validated her feelings. Rather than reply, she wrote a note to herself.

My daughter was born a month ago. She was born via C-Section, which made for a harder recovery.
I gained a lot of weight, and even after delivering an 8lbs baby, I only lost 5lbs.
My husband is not helpful; in fact, he adds stress all the time. My daughter is a sweet girl, but she still gets up every couple of hours at night and only naps for short stints during the day. She falls asleep when she nurses only to wake up an hour later, hungry.

Everything is not going fine. I am not fine. I feel nothing. I'm not happy. Nothing brings me joy. If Jan can feel this way and have a close to an opposite situation from me, I guess it is okay for me to feel this way too. Maybe it is normal, or at least not abnormal.

Chapter Fourteen

Years later, Samantha reflected that not much had changed. There were good weeks with Dr. Jekyll and bad ones with Mr. Hyde. During one of their happier weeks, the couple decided to sell their house and move into a more family-friendly neighborhood, even though it made a much longer commute for Roger. Their new home was located across the street from a fabulous school campus containing the best public elementary, middle, and high schools in the state. As an added bonus, the campus had amazing parks, walking trails, sports fields, and playgrounds. Junior and Sarah, now in fourth and second grade, loved the idea of being able to walk to school. As you drove through their neighborhood, down the magnolia and oak tree-lined boulevard, you would see kids playing in their yards or driveways, riding bikes, and running lemonade stands where the lemonade was either free or to raise money for charity.

The first couple they met was Charlotte and Prescott Callahan. They lived in a beautiful contemporary home around the corner from the Sullivan's. Their home was bright white and looked like it was just power-washed. They had a navy front door and shutters with a deep grey roof. Their yard was neatly manicured, perfectly edged, and was a deep green as if it was artificial turf. The natural areas covered with mulch were weed-free and deep brown as if the mulch was just refreshed. Charming pink flowers wind around the long white front porch railings adding a feminine touch. Not only did their grass seem greener and their house whiter, but their driveway even seemed cleaner.

Charlotte was 5'10 with gorgeous olive skin and long brown hair with natural curls that anyone else would spend hours trying to get those barley curled waves. She had stunning, bright green eyes that seemed to see into your soul. She was the kind of woman you wanted to hate, but that was impossible. She was a caring and empathetic person who always seems to know if you have news, good or bad.

Her husband, Prescott, was bald, 6'4", and very muscular. A patent attorney who is rarely around. He played college football and makes sure everyone knows it. He works a consistent nine-to-five office day, goes to the gym for an hour of weights, an hour of cardio, an hour of basketball, then meets up with co-workers for 'dinner meetings' followed by bar drinking until typically one o'clock in the morning. He's also the kind of person you want to hate, but, in this case, it can be easily accomplished. When they met, he seemed like the best husband and best dad, but how could he be the best with hours like that? Samantha tried not to be judgmental about Prescott since her own husband was so rarely seen that the punchline of jokes at parties was her own 'absentee husband.' Roger was never one for socializing. He could never understand anyone who would go from work to the gym to a bar. He was more of a home-body. He just wanted to come home to his perfect family and relax.

When they first met, Charlotte and Samantha hit it off right away. With their kids being the same age, both women were non-working, stay-at-home moms who liked to volunteer and were often left to parent alone. Roger and Prescott were cordial to each other, but both thought of the other as a pompous ass. Roger uttered that exact phrase about Prescott when they met, and Samantha knew that everyone said that about Roger behind his back.

Charlotte's daughter Bella was the same age as Junior. She had a demanding schedule for a fourth grader. Bella danced competitively and trained three to four hours a day. The dance company also required traveling to competitions most weekends. Her son Ryan was Sarah's age. The two of them were going to be two peas in a pod. They had so much in common and could be the best of friends, that is until he realizes she is a girl.

Friday:

I love our new neighborhood and the neighbors that I have met. They do this thing they call Flamingo Friday. One person has a big plastic flamingo they stake in their front yard on Friday around 5:30pm. The neighbors know that wherever the flamingo is, the party is. As they arrive home from work, they grab their families, head over to the flamingo house, have some snacks, a few drinks, and watch their kids play. Someone takes the flamingo with them to put in their yard the following Friday.

I went to one with Charlotte but am not sure I will ever be brave enough to bring the flamingo home. Charlotte says she never takes it either. Prescott gets home late and doesn't feel that it is appropriate for her to host without him. I cannot imagine the look on Roger's face if he came home only to see dozens of neighbors with their kids running around our yard. I have enough negative comments about being an irresponsible mom, lazy housewife, and too worried about what insignificant people think. I better not go asking for more insults.

Chapter Fifteen

Samantha and Junior had been reading a wizard series together for several years. Samantha always pictured herself as part of one of the houses and loved one of the side characters with her quirky, intellectual, and friendly personality. Junior, of course, wanted to be the main character, so he self-identified as the famous wizard. This Halloween, Samantha helped Junior create a costume so he could go as the cutest wizard you would ever see. Or at least she thought so. She really wanted to be able to walk around with some of the new people from the neighborhood or let Junior Trick-or-Treat with new friends from school, but Sarah still couldn't stay up late and really wanted to hand out candy. With Roger being a no-show for every Halloween since they had kids, Samantha knew she would be solo that evening. With Sarah dressed as a ballerina, Junior as a wizard, and Samantha in her sorcerer t-shirt, they set off with the wagon to take a short walk through the neighborhood before coming back home to pass out candy. Before they left, Samantha placed a classy ceramic pumpkin on the front porch table, filled with chocolate bars and chewy sweets, and a little note saying, "Happy Halloween! Please Take Two Treats!"

As soon as they cleared the driveway, Junior ran to the first house. Sarah had absolutely no interest in going door-to-door, so Samantha pulled her in the wagon with the candy she swiped from their own stash before leaving.

Samantha watched as Junior approached the first door, bravely ringing the doorbell by himself with Samantha and Sarah still out on the neighborhood road. It was not quite dark yet, so it was easy to see him on the front porch from the street. The sweet elderly couple that lived next door that Samantha had only met once answered the door together. They were adorable with the excitement. They went on and on about Junior's costume. It was clear they had no idea who we were dressed as, but they knew he was some familiar character they've seen before. They each grabbed a handful of mini candy bars and threw them in Junior's open bag. He politely thanked them, then looked back with wide eyes at Samantha with a look of amazement that his bag was so full after just one house. He jumped off the couple's front porch and ran through their side yard to get to the next house quicker, and Samantha pulled Sarah further down the street. This went on for several houses before they started running into more crowds. Samantha particularly loved people watching and checking out all the costumes. She could always tell who the really fun parents were by who dressed up and what they dressed up as. There are not a lot of options when it comes to adult costumes for women. The choices are somewhere between inappropriately slutty or scar-your-kids-with-fright scary. There was the occasional mom who didn't care how silly she looked who would wear a blow-up Sumo Wrestler costume or something else, not the slightest bit flattering but certainly entertaining.

A group of teenage girls walked by dressed as different colored chocolates rather than this year's popular risqué sidekick character, and Samantha was reassured that there was hope for future generations. They looked at Sarah and told her how cute she looked as they passed.

Samantha took a break from looking at all of the costumes to check on Junior. It was growing dark fast, and she was getting nervous as she looked around, realizing that it was now much harder to tell one kid from another when so many costumes were dark colors. She glanced up to the house where she thought Junior would be but only saw a crowd of princesses. She looked over to the next house and saw some black capes and hoped Junior was one of them. Just as her heart started to slow, the group turned, and she realized that she was staring at a trio of superheroes. She pulled Sarah faster in the wagon and walked up into the next driveway, scanning the darkness for him. Where was he? Why didn't she dress him as a giant Sumo Wrestler so she could find him easier? She turned in a circle taking in her surroundings; kids running, kids laughing, parents smiling and even drinking. The indistinct noise was happy, but as she spun around in the driveway, everyone looked blurry, and all of the sounds seemed to speed up. Every laugh sounded evil rather than happy; every face she saw was dripping with blood. Things started spinning around her. She tried to take a deep breath noticing Sarah staring at her, concerned. She was getting dizzy, so she sat down on the curb with Sarah next to her in the wagon. She was scared and wanted to curl up, put her head between her knees, and rock herself until someone found Junior and brought him back. But she knew she had to get up and find him, herself. She quickly stood, balanced herself, and turned quickly to the street where she ran right into Charlotte.

"Hi, Samantha!" she said with a big smile. Charlotte looked down at Sarah's chocolate-coated face and hands and said, "Oh, Sarah, don't you look adorable."

"I'm a ballerina," Sarah said between bites of a chocolate bar.

Charlotte looked up at Samantha and noticed her panicked, washed-out face. "Are you okay? You look like you've seen a ghost."

"I can't find Junior. He was right in front of me, and now he's not."

"Oh, he just crossed the street with Bella to hit this one house that gives out king-size candy bars. No worries, they are meeting me back here when they are done."

Samantha breathed for what seemed like the first time since she lost sight of Junior. She smiled at Charlotte, then down at Sarah, and started to chuckle. *Wow, did I overreact or what?* She couldn't believe what a fool she was. This was the safest neighborhood in town, and there were hundreds of parents everywhere. She laughed harder and harder until her eyes teared up. Sarah looked up at Samantha, confused.

"What's so funny, mommy?"

"Ms. Charlotte said I looked like I saw a ghost," she said between laughing fits. "Get it? It's Halloween. There are literally ghosts everywhere." Her hysterical laughter stopped just as Junior and Bella crossed back to their side of the street.

Samantha said goodbye to Charlotte and Bella and made her way home to give out candy with her kids nearby.

"What were you laughing at, mom? I could hear you all the way across the street." Junior said, maybe a bit embarrassed.

"Oh, you had to be there," Samantha said and sighed deeply as if looking back on a fond memory.

"I was there, and I didn't get it." Sarah chimed in, rolling her eyes. When they reached their porch, the huge bowl of candy was now completely empty, and her nice ceramic pumpkin was broken in half on the floor. Before the kids reached the porch, she told them to wait outside and that she would be right back out with popcorn, hot chocolate, and more candy. She grabbed the broken bowl and made her way inside, thankful for the insane amount of candy she bought and thinking back that future generations will likely suck after all.

Chapter Sixteen

Roger waded through the moving boxes in the kitchen that kept getting rearranged from one place to another without getting any emptier. Now a stack, covered with what looked like a garbage bag full of candy, is blocking the coffee machine, so he cursed under his breath and headed out to his car. His car used to calm him. It was his place that he could keep clean and clutter-free, play his music, and just drive. But now that they moved, his commute is significantly longer. He hoped that moving to this neighborhood would bring his old Samantha back, but every morning he questioned if it was worth it. He turned on the radio to listen to sports updates. He didn't recognize the voice talking as the usual morning sports update guy, but it immediately reminded him of that meathead Prescott. The radio guy was arguing that football is not for just anyone and that only real men can play without getting injured. He actually argued that the relationship between football and head trauma was a conspiracy theory. He quickly turned the channel, thinking that he had had enough of hearing those same arguments from Prescott. He only met him once, but he could not get the guy to talk about anything but football in that one time. Even when he walked away to talk to someone else, Roger could hear his booming voice talk to someone else about the exact same thing.

The new channel played music from at least a decade ago, and the song that played brought back memories. He remembered when he and Samantha were dating and how great things were then. She always looked like she just walked out of a salon. She cared about what she looked like and respected her body. Her clothes always looked like they were just bought because she took care of them. She took care of him. He never had to ask for anything. She just knew that if she was making a coffee, he would want one too. She stocked all of his favorite foods in her refrigerator, so he always had what he wanted, even at her house. She made time to keep herself in shape but then didn't spend the rest of the day in her sweat-soaked clothing. Back then, exercise clothes were for exercising, not for the whole day.

The morning show crew talked between songs, and the woman on the show had a sexy laugh. When was the last time that he and Samantha had laughed together? He had forgotten what her laugh even sounded like. He remembered how happy it made him when she smiled and laughed. Her joy was his joy. But she was never happy anymore, and neither was he. What they say must be true, 'If mama ain't happy, nobody's happy.'

Chapter Seventeen

Samantha woke up the most relaxed she could ever remember feeling. It was cool in the room, so the big down comforter was cozy, but the morning sun pouring through the windows made her want to get up. She walked casually over to the bathroom to brush her teeth and could hear the happy sounds of her kids having breakfast. It sounded like they were watching Saturday morning cartoons.

Samantha glanced in the mirror while she was brushing her teeth and noticed how clear her skin looked. Her skin was tight, blemish-free and dewy, her eyes were clear with none of the usual bloodshot red coloring. As she brushed through her hair, it bounced back with a healthy, natural curl. She threw on a sundress that hugged her curves and fit fantastic. After a spritz of perfume, she walked out to the kitchen to join her family.

The kids were talking sweetly, and Roger was at the stove cooking blueberry pancakes. He was humming happily over his work. Samantha saw that there was already a huge platter of pancakes on the table along with syrup, butter, a bowl of fruit salad, and a crystal pitcher of orange juice.

Roger must have noticed she walked in because he stopped humming and told her from the stove to sit down and enjoy her breakfast as he continued to flip pancakes. She was happy to comply, sat down, and noticed the nice cloth napkins were out on the table too. She shook out the napkin, placed it on her lap, checked to see if the kids needed any refills then proceeded to fill her plate.

She couldn't remember the last time she had been so at peace, happy and relaxed. She took a bite of a pancake and savored the flavor of the plump, ripe blueberries as she looked lovingly upon her adorable kids. Before she knew it, Roger had walked up behind her to fill the pancake plate. He leaned over from behind her, kissed her on the cheek, and said, "I love you, my sweet buttercup."

She blushed and smiled, feeling truly loved, with tiny little butterflies in her stomach. It was odd, though; he had never called her 'buttercup' before. It was cute. It reminded her of The Princess Bride. But now that she really thought about it, she didn't realize he knew how to make pancakes. As she stared at her kids enjoying her delicious pancake, she realized how long it had been since she had enjoyed Saturday morning cartoons and had never noticed how often Road Runner made his "beep beep" noises. She turned her attention away from the TV and the kids to thank Roger for the delicious breakfast and peaceful morning.

When he turned from the stove, she was pleasantly surprised to see Ryan Gosling staring back at her, lovingly.

Samantha sat up in bed so fast that she became light-headed. It was still dark outside, and her neighbor's car alarm was going off. She got out of bed to use the bathroom. By the time she returned, the car alarm had stopped. She wandered into the living room, straining to retain the dream. The feeling was still there, barely. Her tummy tickled with love butterflies, the lift of pure happiness, and the comfort of someone who was there to care for her. The details were fading, however. With every passing minute, they grew hazier until the feeling was gone, as well. Now, she did not feel the happiness from the dream. It was replaced with an overwhelming feeling of loss.

Chapter Eighteen

It was difficult juggling two kids while unpacking a new house, but Samantha was feeling great about the move! She thought about finding a new therapist while things have been good, so she has someone to call in case things take a dark turn.

She heard that a new home, or moving in general, were among the top five most stressful events in someone's life. She didn't want to ask friends for therapist recommendations because God forbid anyone from becoming aware that there were troubles with her mental health or, even worse, her marriage. She ran through an online list of therapists in the area, visited their websites, and read their reviews. It seemed like everyone had at least one bad review, but it was pretty easy to detect the trolls as well as the people who just like to complain. She settled on Dr. Pager.

Dr. Pager was a psychiatrist rather than a therapist, counselor, or psychologist, hence the doctor prefix. A visit to her seemed like a good starting place since she could evaluate Samantha's medication and hopefully point her toward a regularly scheduled therapist. Dr. Pager was tall for a woman at just under six feet. She had medium length wavy brown hair and was very approachable. Her office was not only filled with motivational quotes but also funny, crude ones like "If you're honestly happy, fuck what other people think." Samantha instantly relaxed as Dr. Pager lightened the conversation with a liberal sprinkling of curse words. Samantha didn't often curse, at least not in front of her kids. But she was always comfortable around people who could use their language so freely. They spent almost two hours discussing everything currently happening in her life, from the move and friends to her marriage and parenting. She never harped on one specific topic or even suggested a childhood trauma. They discussed her medicine, and Dr. Pager recommended a small change to level things out for her a bit during this time of transition.

Samantha walked out feeling invigorated. She was confident about the future and could not wait to see Dr. Pager again. When she checked out, Samantha was reminded that Dr. Pager is not a therapist. She was only there to evaluate her medication, but if necessary, she would recommend someone for regular counseling. Samantha was bummed out but still refreshed and looked forward to seeing the type of person Dr. Pager would recommend. She tried to picture just the person she would send Samantha to, and for whatever reason, she pictured a topless Lenny Kravitz from his long, dreadlocks days, stretched out on a sofa, nursing a cocktail.

Thursday:

Met with Dr. Pager today. She is absolutely amazing. My deep dive into my mental state continued after the appointment; that's when I realized something.

- *When I get in the car, I have to turn on the radio*
- *When I go to bed at night, I read until I fall asleep with the book in my hand*
- *If I have a few minutes or more of downtime, I have to pick up my phone, turn on the TV, or work on a puzzle*

It just became clear that I cannot be alone with myself. I cannot even remember the last time I sat down and just thought about life, about my past, about my future. I am afraid of where my mind will go. I know there have been times when just thinking about my panic attack will make me remember the fear, feel the fear, and maybe even...

I cut off my last sentence to play solitaire on my phone. When I am distracted on my phone, my head is right because it is occupied and not caught up in thoughts that will make me think of...

Tomorrow is Flamingo Friday! I have a cute outfit picked out and feel okay about going solo. I know Roger will be working late, but that's fine. I will bring my famous seven-layer dip. Nothing makes a powerful first impression like a good dip.

Chapter Nineteen

Junior and Sarah rode their bikes while Samantha walked over to Leslie's house around the corner. Samantha met Leslie on a walk through the neighborhood a couple days ago and realized their sons were the same age. Leslie also had a three-month-old Aussie-Doodle puppy that Sarah could not get enough of. They approached Leslie's house. Her front yard was covered in plastic flamingos and, for some reason, a big blow-up snow globe. She walked up the driveway to where a group of men was gathering. As Samantha approached, she recognized Prescott. He had everyone's undivided attention as he told a story about 'knocking the snot out of some poor sap who didn't belong on the football field.' Samantha thought of walking up to the group, but her palms were sweaty, and she had no idea what to say. She couldn't imagine herself being able to look entertained or impressed by Prescott's good-ole-days of football stories. The women had to be inside. She sent Junior and Sarah to play in the backyard with the other kids and headed into the house to find the women.

Leslie was at the counter with three other ladies. They were all talking about how great her remodeled kitchen had turned out. As Samantha approached the kitchen, Leslie greeted her and introduced her to the group. They told her about a neighborhood club that meets once a month to play Bunco, a dice game that mostly consisted of talking, drinking, and mindlessly throwing dice. Another woman whose name she immediately forgot said they also have a book club that gets together once a month, where they pick a book, everyone starts it, no one finishes it, and they get together to drink and laugh about how no one read it. The women all laughed and began telling stories about the crazy things that happened at these get-togethers. Samantha quietly excused herself to use the bathroom. She stood in front of the mirror in the hallway half bathroom and stared at her reflection. What was she doing there? Roger would never come to one of these with her, and he certainly would not approve of her getting together with a group of crazy drinking moms multiple times a month. She couldn't relate to the stories the women talked about when Leslie recommended a trashy, romantic novel for book club any more than she could relate to Prescott's tackling tales. Just then, she realized that she hadn't seen Charlotte. Surely, she would feel more comfortable with the one person she was really getting to know.

She walked out of the bathroom and peeked out at the kids in the backyard. She only saw Charlotte's son, which reminded her that Charlotte was away at a dance competition with her daughter. That certainly explained Prescott's rare appearance. She debated walking out the back door, grabbing the kids, and slipping out the side gate but thought it best to act like an adult and not pull a runner.

Leslie approached Samantha with a drink as she walked back into the kitchen.

"Thank you, Leslie. But Roger just called and needs me to meet him at home to help him with something." Samantha realized what a horribly weak excuse that was and hoped Leslie would not ask for more information.

"Oh, no. We are just getting started, girl! Is it okay if your kids stay a little longer? I can send them home after hot dogs if that's okay. That will give you plenty of time to "help Roger'" she said with a sly grin and finger quotes.

Samantha thanked her and began her walk back home alone, wondering what kind of crazy tales would be spun about her when she left.

Chapter Twenty

Monday morning, after Samantha walked with the kids out the front door and watched them begin their walk to school together, she sat down and checked her schedule. Nothing. She had plans to get a pedicure, but Charlotte canceled last night because she and her daughter caught a stomach bug at the dance competition, and Samantha did not want to go alone. She had no plans and nothing to do until the kids got home, so she stripped out of her clothes and climbed back in bed. She rolled onto her side, took a deep, cleansing breath, closed her eyes, and the phone rang.

Samantha planned to screen out the call, but when she glanced at the Caller ID, with her finger hovering over the decline button, she saw the call was coming from school. She quickly answered the call.

"Hello, this is Samantha Sullivan," she answered in an oddly professional voice that she had not used in years.

"Good morning, Mrs. Sullivan. This is Mr. Small, the principal over at Taft Elementary."

"Hi. Is everything okay? Are Junior and Sarah okay?"

He chuckled, "Yes. I apologize. I should have started with that. Most people do seem to get startled when they get a call from the school." He chuckled again, then continued. "I am calling, first and foremost, to welcome you and your family to our school. Your children's teachers say Roger and Samantha fit right in."

Samantha cringed at the awkwardness. She knew they were new to the school, but shouldn't he know Roger went by Junior if he talked to the teachers? She just chalked up the secondary flub because Sarah and Samantha both start with an S, and maybe he was confused because Samantha was the one on the phone with him. She shook it off and replied, "Thank you. I am sorry that I have not been in to meet you yet."

"Nothing to be sorry about. Chances are we would miss each other if you had just popped in, anyway," he replied dismissively.

His welcome faded into the vaguely familiar feeling of not being good enough or deserving his time.

"We are reaching out to some of our younger parents, or in your case, new parents to our school." he scoffed. "We would like to invite you to volunteer with a class once a week to help us with some of the children who need a bit of extra assistance."

Thanks for the invitation, she wanted to say, but instead said, "I am happy to help. Would I be helping in my own children's classrooms?"

"Actually, we plan to place volunteers where we have the biggest need. Thanks for being flexible. Our volunteer coordinator will contact you to schedule a time to come by the school and get set up. Bye."

Before she had time to process, argue, or even say goodbye herself, he hung up.

***

Roger was in a good mood when he arrived home that evening. Samantha sat with him while he ate his dinner and told him about her call with the principal.

"His kindness was so fake, and he was so dismissive," she said to Roger after detailing her call with Mr. Small.

"Oh, give him a break. He probably has to deal with stay-at-home moms all day. He has to pretend that he likes you, but he doesn't really have to enjoy it, does he?"

"If you had to talk to me all day, would that be so bad?" she asked, her feelings clearly hurt.

"Honestly? I work so hard all day. I answer to the CEO and Board of Directors, neither of which seem to know anything about what I do. They don't know what questions to ask, let alone the answers. I try to explain how things work in my sector in the simplest way I can, but they are all clueless. These are brilliant men who have built and managed successful companies most of their adult life. I feel for Mr. Small. Having to explain myself to a woman who doesn't even work would be so belittling."

"It's not as if I was questioning his methods. He is the one who called me asking for my help," she said, raising her voice just slightly.

"He probably had to make that call. I'm sure he had other more pressing tasks on his agenda, but courtesy and the need for volunteers dictated he needed to make that call. It sounded like he was cordial enough. He welcomed us to the school and asked for help. What is the big deal?" he asked as he stood and left the room, leaving his dirty plates on the table for Samantha to clean up.

Chapter Twenty-One

A couple days later, Samantha sat on the front porch waiting for Junior and Sarah to come home. After having a productive day reorganizing her closet and changing the sheets on all of the beds, she was in a great mood. She was most excited that Roger was away on a business trip, and she had a fun evening planned for her and the kids.

She remembered feeling this excited for Roger to come home when he had been out of town for work. Sometimes even when they both worked late after a long day and she arrived home first, she would grab two glasses of wine and wait for him on the front porch or in the kitchen, ready to pounce when he walked through the door. They both worked hard, and the anticipation of seeing each other again grew stronger as the daily hours waned.

What has changed in their marriage? What was different now? They have two kids, and he is constantly on edge because of work, but many couples go through the same. Where she once upon a time could not wait to see him at the end of the day, she now cherished the evenings she slept alone when he was out of town and dreaded the hour when he came home to ruin their evening when he came home from work.

It saddened her and made her think of what changed; when was it that everything changed? Why couldn't things be the way they were before? Would things between them improve as their kids grew older and the more she evolved into her role? What if it took her until the kids went off to college for her to go back to her old personality, her old way of doing things, and feel like her old self again? By then, it would be too late. She and Roger would not even know each other anymore.

She saw the kids cross the street to their neighborhood and shook off the depressing thoughts. Tonight will be awesome. Yes, it will be awesome because Roger is not home, but she will have to deal with that later. Tonight is her time with her kids, and she planned to enjoy every minute of it.

When the kids walked into the yard, they smiled, excited to see their mom waiting for them. Sarah dropped her backpack and ran to give Samantha a big hug. Junior picked up Sarah's bag and carried both of their things inside, but only after stopping to get a kiss on the cheek from Samantha at the door. The three of them had only just entered the house when Junior looked at Sarah, and they both shouted, "Cookies!!!" The smell of fresh-baked cookies filled the house, everything was tidy and clean, and even the windows were spotless as the bright afternoon sun lit up their home.

Samantha trailed her kids into the kitchen and poured three large milk glasses for them to enjoy with their cookies. Usually, she would put one or two small cookies on a plate for each of them and store the rest before the kids even got home, but today there was excitement in the air, like a holiday, so she left the whole batch piled festively on a plate.

Listening to the kids talk about their day always brought a smile to Samantha's face. Listening to the long, drawn-out stories, some of which with absolutely no point, was enjoyable to her when she had the time to appreciate their voices, facial expressions, and the fact that they would just keep going because they just want to talk to her.

The kids finished their cookies and ran off to work on their homework while Samantha stayed in the kitchen and cleaned up. She washed the dishes while thinking about what they would do that evening. She planned to order pizza. They could play a board game or two, then find a good movie to watch. She sighed, thinking about how her plans sounded like the perfect evening.

She got startled when her cell phone rang. Samantha dried her hands and looked at the Caller ID. It was Leslie from down the street. "Hey, girl! It's Leslie."

"Hi, Leslie. How are you doing?"

"Great. Hey, look. We are short a player for Bunco tonight. Charlotte suggested you, and I thought that was a fabulous idea. Are you available around sevenish? I am picking up a catering pack from Nacho Mama's Cooking and will have plenty of wine. All you have to bring is yourself and five dollars."

Samantha thought it sounded fun, and Roger wouldn't really have to know. She hated to think of bailing on her fun night with the kids, but she hadn't even told them her plans yet. "Oh, that sounds fun!" Then she remembered, "But, Roger is out of town, and I don't even know where to find a babysitter with this late notice."

"No worries. My niece, Beth, is in town. She is thinking of moving here. She is twenty-two, responsible, and has no interest in hanging around a bunch of drunk moms tonight. Why don't I send her down at 6:45, so you can meet her and get her settled in?"

Samantha thanked her and continued to get everything organized for a fun night with no real excuse left. Only this fun night for her kids didn't involve her anymore. She organized the games, found a good movie, and ordered pizza for when Beth arrived.

A few hours later, Samantha was dressed in an old pair of slightly distressed jeans, a light grey V-neck T-shirt, and flip-flops. She curled her hair into beachy waves, then added a swipe of mascara and her diamond stud earrings. The pizza had just arrived, and Beth was getting the kids fed in the kitchen. Beth was just as Leslie had described. Samantha's first impression was that she seemed very responsible, kind, and also looked like she would really be fun for the kids, not on her phone the whole time. She had very short-cropped black hair and seemingly flawless mocha skin. She brought a backpack full of games and magic tricks for the kids, and her computer for after the kids went to bed. She knew all the right questions to ask. Where are the bathrooms? What time do you want the kids in bed? What is their bedtime routine? When do you expect to be home? Samantha could hardly think of anything else to tell her when she left since Beth already asked for all of the information she needed. Samantha turned on the outside lights, kissed the kids, said goodbye, and locked the doors, feeling confident about the night ahead for both her kids and herself.

Samantha walked to Leslie's house but was surprised by how many cars were parked in the cul-de-sac considering this was a neighborhood group. She arrived at the door at 7:10, feeling horrible for being late. Roger had lectured her several times about how certain circumstances require you to be on time, like interviews, meetings, and to catch a flight. But he stressed that at other times like parties or neighborhood get-togethers, it is actually rude to be early or on-time. It always stressed her out to show up late, but she didn't want to be the weird friend who showed up first while the host was still prepping, as was usually the case. She was certainly not the first person here, though. From the look of it, she may be the last, or maybe even got the time wrong.

She stood at the door and rang the doorbell. The large, double front doors were made of wood and glass, so she could see straight through to the kitchen where all the women were congregating. The music and laughter were so loud that it didn't seem that anyone heard the doorbell. She tried the door handle; it was unlocked. She let herself in. Leslie walked past the door with a little dance in her step, and she saw Samantha out of the corner of her eye.

"Hey, look who's here!" Leslie yelled over the music as she slowly danced her way to the front door. She gave Samantha a little hip bump, invited her in, and went to get her a drink.

In Leslie's beautiful, new, state-of-the-art kitchen, she had prepared a spread that could be featured on the cover of Coastal Living magazine. Across one counter there were at least fifty bottles of wine. When Samantha walked over to them, she noted that the countertop was somehow chilled, so the wine was the perfect temperature. There was a large clear-view refrigerator next to the counter, which on one side held an assortment of beer and on the other an elaborate collection of vintage wines. There was a multilevel bar filled with top-shelf liquor that looked like it belonged at a posh night club to one side of her. To the other side was a large, presumably, custom-made farm table covered with an enormous nacho bar. As she took in the incredible assortment of offerings, Leslie approached her again, this time holding a giant, frozen margarita with a cute tag on the stem of the glass that said, "Mommy's Sippy Cup." Samantha didn't know how it didn't spill everywhere, as much as Leslie was dancing, in addition to holding her own drink. Samantha thanked her and took a sip of the delicious concoction, that Leslie described as her 'Slushy Lushy' recipe, and walked around to find Charlotte.

Samantha was already tipsy after only a couple of long sips but still managed to locate Charlotte out back by the pool where the card tables were set up. The back porch had a full-sized refrigerator packed with water, juice pouches, wine spritzers, and even more beer. There was a large, flat-screen TV on the wall that looked to be the source of the music that was, in turn, piped throughout the house speakers. She walked down the wide deck stairs to the pool, where she found a shuffleboard court, luxury hotel-type lounge chairs, and a fire pit. This was like a vacation house for an MTV party or an episode of Cribs. Charlotte saw Samantha and waved her over to the table where she was sitting. Samantha gave her a hug and a silent hello as someone she remembered meeting on Flamingo Friday was in the middle of a story. She was a forgettable person, who Samantha had no inclination to get to know better, but as she carried on, she remembered her name was Georgia.

"So, George, ball-tapped him with his beer bottle, and Prescott dropped his shoulder and drove it into his stomach and pinned him against the side of the house." she laughed then continued, "Six months later, his ribs are finally healed, and he learned the lesson about ball-tapping that he should've learned back in college."

Seriously, George and Georgia? She held in a laugh so as not to give her the impression that her story was funny. Even Charlotte only smiled out of courtesy, but Samantha knew she was embarrassed with the retelling of a story she would clearly like to forget.

A look of relief washed across Charlotte's face as Leslie cut the music and ushered the rest of the indoor crowd out to the tables around the pool. She quickly reviewed the rules of the game for everyone, then cranked the music back up and began placing delectable treats on every table as well as getting drink refills for those who needed one.

"Is Leslie not playing?" Samantha asked.

"The host never plays. Their job is to provide food, drinks, and entertainment. You picked the right month to come to Bunco. Leslie is the best host. It will not be this elaborate every month." Charlotte replied.

"Thanks to you, Charlotte! Thanks for suggesting that Leslie invite me. I am not sure I completely understand the game, but it is great to get out of the house or even to be wearing real clothes after 8pm." Samantha smiled and the whole table laughed, except Georgia.

"There is really nothing to understand." Georgia butted in. "Everyone else here has played before, so any partner you have will know how to keep score. You can just roll the dice. It is totally mindless. No skill involved. You just roll the dice, eat, drink, and gossip." She probably meant to make Samantha feel better, but the way she said it actually made her feel like an idiot for not really understanding.

Charlotte and her partner won the first game, so the two of them had to move tables. When Charlotte stood, Samantha saw how cute she was dressed. She was wearing tiny, white shorts and incredible Jimmy Choo stilettos, both of which showed off her long, tanned legs. On top, she wore an orange, crisscrossed halter top that made her skin glow. Samantha recognized that she was staring when the ladies at her table tried to get her attention to start the next round. She reached for her margarita, which was suddenly full with a new little umbrella and cherry on top. She had no idea how much she was actually drinking because each time she turned around, Leslie magically snuck up and topped her off. Samantha looked around to locate Leslie so she could thank her but saw that she was now straddling the top ledge of the fire pit, which thankfully was not lit, and was twerking, sort of.

Her attention turned back to the table as Georgia started talking about her "smoking hot trainer" at the gym. She glanced over to Samantha, looked her up and down, and said, "You don't go to a gym, Samantha, do you?"

Samantha felt the need to explain why she didn't belong to a gym or tell them what she did for exercise, or even justify to these women that she was actually a very talented athlete in her youth despite her current body. Instead, she just picked up the dice, rolled, and replied "No."

"Well, I have been working with Tony, and he is amazing. He said I have been doing such a great job that he gave me a few guest passes. I think I have them with me." She stopped, reached under the table, nearly knocking her wine over, dug into her purse, pulling out a gym pass the size of a business card. She handed it over to Samantha. "Here. You can work out for free for two weeks and get two personal training sessions with Tony as a trial. You will love it. Everyone works out there. It is super social as much as anything else."

Samantha thanked her and pocketed the gym pass just as Georgia rolled the dice right off the table.

Before she knew it, it was eleven o'clock at night on a Tuesday. Samantha could not remember the last time she stayed out this late, especially on a weeknight without Roger. The game had ended. Some women remained seated at their tables, yawning, but most were up and dancing around the pool or fire pit. A couple women were playing shuffleboard with pine cones, and she could hear them debating on jumping into the pool. She decided it was time for her to get home, relieve Beth, and get herself to bed. She tried to wave a thank you and goodbye to Leslie, who was still dancing somehow, but she was in the zone and not to be disturbed. On her way back through the house,

Samantha ran into Charlotte, who was stepping out of the bathroom. She didn't seem drunk but was glowing, probably from a buzz. She said she wouldn't likely stay much longer since she was meeting with her running group at 5:30 the next morning. Charlotte gave her a warm hug and walked back outside to rejoin the party.

Samantha arrived home to find Beth sitting at the kitchen table on her computer. Samantha paid her, and in turn, Beth handed her a report of everything Junior and Sarah ate and everything they did. Samantha begged Beth to move to town. Beth just chuckled, surely noticing that Samantha had overindulged and said that she was fine to walk back to Leslie's house on her own. Samantha called a quick warning to her as she walked down the driveway that there were still many drunk women at her aunt's house, and it seemed to be only getting crazier.

Samantha kicked off her flip flops, grabbed a bottle of water, tugged off her shirt, and walked out of her jeans without stopping on her path to the bedroom. She walked right toward her bed and fell face-first onto her pillow, wearing only her bra and panties.

Chapter Twenty-Two

Charlotte tossed and turned all night. By four in the morning, and after a couple grunts from Prescott's side of the bed, she decided she may as well get up. Her endocrinologist had changed her Diabetes regimen a few weeks ago. It caused her weight to fluctuate, and she has not been sleeping well since. She used to complain to her friends and family about her diagnosis and how difficult it was to live with a chronic illness. But as she got older, she took a step back and realized the problems other people have to deal with were often way worse and started to keep her disease to herself.

She made herself a coffee and sat down with a book on the back porch. She read the same page repeatedly because her mind was still on Bunco from last night. Charlotte didn't drink but didn't like having to explain herself to others, so she always showed up with a large tumbler of San Pellegrino with a splash of cranberry juice and a lime. Charlotte's parents are both sober after years of being alcoholics. She saw first-hand what alcoholism can do to a marriage, a family, and the body. She vowed early in life to just stay away from it altogether. In her early twenties, she noticed that saying you don't drink can often come across like a vegan telling a carnivore that they don't eat meat. Thankfully, no one ever asked her what she was drinking. But last night Leslie grabbed her drink, took a big swig, and then made a face like it was a tequila shot. The thought made her giggle. Leslie was a riot.

After realizing she was not getting anywhere in her book, she decided to be productive. She dressed for the run she had with her training group, which was actually not too long from now. By the time she packed book bags, signed field trip papers, made lunches, and breakfast for the kids, it was time for her to go. She quietly closed the door behind her and walked the mile to where the group met at the coffee shop down the street. As she passed Samantha's house, she thought that she should invite her to start joining the group for these runs. But, when she recalled mentioning it to her last night, Samantha did not look the slightest bit interested. Maybe it was just because it was late and she had been drinking. Mornings give everything a fresh perspective. She would invite her later. Moving is tough and getting involved is the best way to make a new place your home.

Chapter Twenty-Three

Samantha woke up to the morning sun shining through the sheer white curtains covering her windows. The ceiling fan above her bed moved so slow that it almost made her fall back to sleep. She swung her legs over the side of the bed and noticed she had fallen asleep in her clothes from the previous night. She looked down and saw her petite white shorts on her long and lean legs. She saw her lush brown hair fall over her shoulder out of the corner of her eye, then she looked down at her bright orange top. She stepped onto the floor and picked up her very expensive high heels, and stared into the mirror as "I'm Still Standing" played on the radio in the background. Samantha stood frozen, shocked, yet pleased to see that it was Charlotte who stared back.

Chapter Twenty-Four

Samantha awoke to her alarm, set to a station playing an Elton John marathon. Sarah was cuddled up next to her. She didn't remember her coming into the room but enjoyed it none-the-less. She snoozed her alarm to give them a few more minutes of quiet snuggles and with the hope that this odd sensation of having fur growing in her mouth would go away.

After swallowing a few pills for her headache and taking a shockingly cold shower, she was able to get the kids prepared for school and get breakfast ready. For every uncomfortably hungover moment, she reminded herself that she could go right back to bed after the kids left for school. Her cell phone rang on the counter by the door where she left it last night when she arrived home. Junior walked by, saw it was Roger, and answered it. Samantha stood next to him, waiting for him to pass the phone, but he just stared at it then put it down. "Battery is dead, mom," he said as he grabbed his lunch went about packing it into his big backpack.

"Did dad say anything?" she asked Junior as he took off out the door.

"He said he took an early flight back and will be home in about fifteen minutes. Then the phone died. Bye, mom!" and he and Sarah walked to school.

Fifteen minutes? She had a throbbing hangover and was certain that despite her shower, she smelled of margaritas. Her shirt and jeans were still sitting on the floor from where she stripped them off the night before. Samantha chugged down her coffee, smacked herself in the face a couple times, and got to the tasks of getting the kitchen cleaned up, beds made, all of her night out evidence put away. Roger walked in as she was starting a load of laundry.

"How was your trip?" she asked in a voice a little too chipper to be sincere.

"Did Junior hang up on me? I tried calling back, no one answered. Is something wrong, or did he hang up on me?" Either way, he was angry, and she knew it.

"I'm sorry, but my phone battery died right after he answered. We are all excited that you are back early, though."

He squinted at her as if he was trying to see through the lies. He sniffed the air, looked around, like he was looking for clues, then back to her. "What's going on?"

"Nothing at all." She walked over, kissed his cheek, then continued, "Just a normal day. I am starting a load of laundry, then am heading over to volunteer at school. Will you be here all day?"

"I am just here to drop off my things and take a quick shower. I guess I will see you tonight," he said, still looking around suspiciously.

Samantha grabbed her journal, water, purse, and ran out to her car. She knew she was not approved to volunteer at the school yet, but she had to get out of the house. She may as well have a bright, neon sign that said 'LIAR' over her head, and if she stayed one minute longer, he would know she went to play Bunco with the women that he "did not think would be good influences on her."

She drove to the community park on the school campus across the street. There were a few young moms with toddlers on the playground, some people playing tennis, and about a dozen people with dogs, but thankfully no cars in the parking lot by the softball fields. She parked, unrolled the windows, put her chair back, and took a much-needed nap. It's hard work being a double agent, party girl.

Wednesday:

I am torn on whether I should tell Roger that I went to Bunco last night. I know he will be mad, but it is nothing next to how mad he would be if he found out from someone else or from the kids. If I explained to him that they needed a sub and that Leslie's niece was available to babysit, he would understand. I was just helping them out this once, right? It's not like I left the kids alone, and I was only down the street. I had fun and would like to do it again, but I don't think I can continue to do it behind Roger's back.

I am amazed at how open these women are with each other. One woman very openly talked about how she caught her husband in an affair. Another woman told vivid accounts of her menopausal journey. Leslie told everyone that she was concerned that her son was only nine and was already sprouting pubic hair. I cannot imagine knowing anyone well enough to share anything even close to that personal. I don't even think I could confess to them that I told Roger I went to volunteer, only to take a nap in the park. I enjoy talking about the good things in life, but last night was a venting of problems for everyone. It's bad enough that I went. If I aired my dirty laundry as they did, Roger would never forgive me.

Chapter Twenty-Five

After a wasted, hungover day, Samantha awoke the next morning feeling motivated to get something done. She still did not have her volunteer appointment at school, so she decided to go through her jeans pockets, still balled up on the floor, and fish out the gym pass Georgia had given her. She slid on her athletic shorts, a sports bra, and t-shirt and put her hair up in a ponytail.

When she walked through the front door of the gym, she immediately felt out of place. This wasn't the kind of gym she was used to. She was accustomed to a gym where you could hit the treadmill or elliptical, lift weights, and be done. This place was more like a spa. She stood in the entryway and took in her surroundings. To the right was a full sushi restaurant. To the left was an actual spa with hairdressers at the front and signs advertising facial and massage services at the back. On the second floor, which was open to the foyer where she was standing, she saw a huge aerobics class, with high BPM tracks pumping out at max volume and everyone seemingly gyrating in sync. Directly in front of her was the front desk, where two beautiful twins with long blond hair, crop tops, and tiny little shorts were staring at her with fake, plastic smiles. "Can we help you?" they said together. Samantha looked around, feeling like she was being punked.

"I got this guest pass from a friend." Samantha started, and immediately one of the twins walked around the desk to shake her hand and welcome her.

"Thank you for coming in to give us a try. My name is Jenna, and this is my sister Jana. I have some paperwork for you to fill out, then I would be happy to give you a full tour and get you scheduled for your first training session with Tony." Samantha sat down at a booth in the cafe located directly behind the front desk.

She had a hard time concentrating on what she was doing because the people watching was so interesting. Every woman that walked by seemed to place fashion over function and looked like they fixed their hair before coming in. She wondered how they could exercise and sweat with their hair down like that. But the more she watched, the less she believed these women actually worked out at all. She eavesdropped on two young moms at the table next to her who clearly were just there to have a peaceful lunch and massage while their kids went to the free childcare.

She saw a large built man in a tank top surrounded by at least four women in the distance. The women seemed star-struck by this guy. Even the men would walk by and try to make eye contact with him. Just as Samantha started to wonder who this guy was that deserved all this attention, he turned around, and she saw his face. It was Prescott. She knew from listening to Prescott's stories that he was a big-time football player, but from what Georgia told her last night at Bunco, he is a bit of a local celebrity from his days of playing high school and college ball right here in town. He started walking towards the cafe, so Samantha, in no mood to talk with him, put her head down, and finished filling out her form.

Jenna/Jana came back and led her on a tour of the facility. She wouldn't be surprised if this place had its own zip code. Everything was so big, so luxurious, so clean, it was unlike any gym she had ever been to or even imagined. They walked through the locker rooms to the indoor and then the outdoor pools. She saw Prescott every place they toured. She saw him again at the outdoor pool, sipping a smoothie and talking with some friends.

Samantha remembered going to the gym in college. She would go to the gym to train, to lift, to better herself. She never went to socialize. She remembered what it would feel like to feel the envious stares of 'regular' students when she and her fellow student-athletes would walk by. She didn't let it go to her head, nor did she really care, but the stares she was getting now are more of pity with mild adoration. A bit like, "Oh, you aging chunky mom. Good for you for getting off your ass and getting to the gym."

When they walked back through the locker room, she noticed several saunas and steam rooms. Each shower was draped with huge, high-quality bath sheets, stocked with spa-quality shampoo, conditioner, shaving cream, fresh razors, and soap. She also couldn't help but notice that most women didn't see a need to use the nice bath sheets and just dried their hair in front of the mirror butt naked. She supposed if she had a figure like they did, she would want to show it off too.

Jenna/Jana left to find Tony the Trainer, and Samantha walked out of the locker room and headed up to the cardio floor to check out the treadmills. She walked right into Prescott and a new group of followers as she turned the corner. He was again, just chatting and sipping his bottomless smoothie. She wondered to herself when he found the time to actually work out or if there was something suspect in those protein shakes.

"Hey, Samantha. Did you guys join here?" he asked.

"I am here on a guest pass, just checking it out."

"You should get Roger in here to see the place too. I got the feeling he wouldn't be too keen on our country club, but I bet he would dig this place. We play pick-up basketball on Saturday mornings if he wants in."

"It is nice here. I didn't think of it this morning, but I should've asked Charlotte to come with me," she said in hindsight.

Prescott chuckled and said, "Well, good luck with that."

Samantha had heard that tone before from Roger. Did Prescott not think Charlotte was good enough? Was he insinuating that she wouldn't show up at the gym or that she doesn't exercise enough? "What are you talking about?" Samantha asked a bit too aggressively, eyeing the women and a couple of guys surrounding him. "Your wife is in great shape. If I didn't know better, I would think she comes at least a couple times a week."

"You have me all wrong, Samantha. I said that because she comes here before the kids go to school to squeeze in her two-hour workout. Well, when she doesn't have her running group anyway."

Samantha's face burned hot, feeling foolish. Not every husband doubted his wife. She should have known that Charlotte worked out so much. Samantha forced a smile, said goodbye, and walked back to the locker room, hoping to head home and hide.

On her way out, Jenna/Jana walked up to her with a very muscular man with a shaved head and dark ebony skin. He smiled with his white teeth, hazel eyes and dimples, making her stomach flip. "You must be Tony. I'm Samantha," she said. "I've heard quite a lot about you from Georgia. Thanks for the gym pass, by-the-way."

"It's great to meet you, Samantha. I can tell by looking at you that you are a competitive athlete," he said, somehow looking sincere. She was unsure what caught his eye to bring him to this conclusion, her double chin, her spare tire, her floppy triceps, or her thick ankles. Either way, she was flattered and started to blush.

"I used to play D1 soccer, but it's been a long time."

"Nonsense. Once an athlete, always an athlete." Tony said with a smile.

The two talked for about half an hour about her goals, background, and familiarity with gym equipment. After Tony scheduled her to come in later that week and left to meet his next appointment, Samantha left the gym feeling more confident than she had been in years. She understood why Georgia talked about Tony in such high regard. Yes, he is attractive, but he had the unique ability to make you feel special and worthy.

Chapter Twenty-Six

Samantha's volunteer appointment arrived the following day. She walked into Taft Elementary School for the first time since she registered her kids to switch schools. She was amazed at the bureaucracy to just be allowed to talk to a student on campus. She knew it was for security, but it seemed like too many hoops to jump through to help out. First, she had to sign in to the computer in the office. It took longer the first time because she had to fill out a parent volunteer application. She finished filling out all of her information when an alert popped up letting her know she could not be around any student or teacher until her background check was returned (and she presumed, cleared). She checked the box, granting permission for them to run her background check.

Next, she was taken to a presentation titled 'Volunteer Contract.' She flipped through the slides feeling like most of it was common sense, and she couldn't believe she had to sit through it.... no touching the students, no inappropriate language, no getting involved in student discipline, no outside food or drinks allowed, detailed logs must be kept for every visit including the time in - time out - teacher - classroom location - and the students' specific names she personally interacted with. That last one was a bit much, but after all of the other steps she had been through already, it was not a surprise. She then read the dress code and saw that yoga pants, cotton T-Shirts, and jeans were not allowed, and neither were flip flops. This was her entire wardrobe! What in the world was she supposed to wear. The only other item in her closet was a formal dress she wore to Roger's work gala. She continued reading and saw that the next bullet point was that cell phones were not allowed in the building... she understood that in a way, with photos and distractions, but only agreed to it since her kids were both at that school. She would feel so naked being somewhere without her children and knowing no-one could reach her.

She begrudgingly signed the volunteer contract then continued to the next slide that unexpectedly had a link to a test she had to pass. Had she paid enough attention during the slides, or was she so irritated in having to do all of this busywork that she flipped through it too fast? What happened if she didn't pass? Would they let her do it again, or would she be banned from school? Do they have a wall full of pictures of all the parents who failed their parent volunteer test? Even if they let her retake it, would the principal know she was the woman who didn't pass the first time? She read the first question:

Which of the following is an appropriate interaction between a parent volunteer and a student:

    A. Assisting in the bathroom

    B. Hugging

    C. Texting

    D. Answering questions about classwork

She was much more relaxed after answering the first one and was quickly made aware that all of the questions were similarly obvious.

- *Are you allowed to take photos of students and post them on social media or photo share websites?*
- *Should you cancel your volunteer appointment if you are sick?*
- *Can you discipline a child who is not following directions?*
- *If you think a teacher is teaching something incorrectly, should you correct him/her in front of the class?*
- *Is it okay to talk about students with other parents or friends?*
- *Should volunteers use the student or staff bathrooms?*

She actually wasn't entirely sure about the last one. It made sense for volunteers to stay out of the student bathrooms, but would they be intruding if they went to the staff bathrooms? Can volunteers go to the staff lounge too? Shouldn't that be private for them?

A cheesy picture of a kitty wearing a pink party hat with her paws up in the air, surrounded by balloons and confetti, appeared with a message letting Samantha know she passed. She was relieved and even felt accomplished. She hoped they would give her a sticker on the way out like the 'I Voted' ones you get on election day, that she could wear all day to show off her achievement.

Thursday:

I finally met our esteemed principal today. He was in the office when I signed in for volunteering. We had only spoken briefly on the phone, so I didn't expect him to know me. I approached him and introduced myself. He smiled and shook my hand, clearly searching his mind database for my information. My name didn't even seem to ring a bell. He told me he was SO thankful for all of the volunteers and quickly removed himself from the situation. He breezed through the room like a politician, afraid if he stayed too long, someone would ask him a question he didn't want to answer. Cordial, my ass.

Chapter Twenty-Seven

Samantha remembered that she was scheduled for her first personal training session with Tony today. She wanted to get some exercise but just didn't feel up for getting her ass kicked by a trainer. She called the gym and left a message for Tony, letting him know that she was not feeling well and would call to reschedule. But to make sure the morning was not a waste, she threw on her sneakers and headed out the front door for a walk. She put in her earbuds, turned on some good workout music, and had walked just less than a quarter-mile when she passed the neighborhood coffee shop. Seeing a couple sitting outside drinking their coffee reminded her that she had not had her coffee this morning and decided to grab a cup to go.

Samantha walked up to the counter to place her order as a chill crept up her spine along with the pressure of being watched. She looked out of the corner of her eye to see who was staring. It was two beautiful, young women dressed smartly in skirt suits. After she placed her order, she drifted off to the corner to wait. She could hear the women talking and could feel their stare. They either thought she had music playing in her headphones or just didn't care.

"That, is Roger's wife? You are joking, right?"

"Totally serious! I saw her picture in his office. That is for sure her."

"But he is such a catch. He has to be loaded and is good looking for an older guy. Why would he be with her when he can have his pick of any woman at work?"

So that was it. Samantha put together that these must be the hot admins that she had heard other executives talk about. Normally, this would bother her, but she just wanted to throw hot coffee in their faces. They gave her one last glance and walked out while Samantha stared at them from behind, imagining how fun it would be if one of them tripped.

"Samantha." the barista called.

Samantha walked up to the teenager at the counter who looked too young to be working, thanked her for the coffee, and asked her to add a box of a dozen donuts to her order. Over the last five minutes, she had successfully talked herself out of her walk, but now she had to figure out how to walk home without being seen carrying a box of donuts. As she left the coffee shop, thinking of how to best conceal her box, she wasn't watching where she was going and ran right into Tony, who had just pulled into the parking lot to grab a coffee.

"Hi, Samantha. I got your message. Are you feeling any better?" he said, without a hint of suspicion, which just made her mad. Shouldn't he knock the donuts out of her hand and tell her to get her shit together instead of staring at her sympathetically and completely avoiding the donuts with his eyes?

"Yes. Thanks. I just had to pick up... some things. I am heading home now to rest."

"I hope you feel better. Drink lots of water, okay?"

She was tempted to dump the box of donuts into the trash bin, but that would be wasteful. She grew up with her mom telling her about all the starving kids in Africa, after all.

Friday:
Charlotte called today to invite me to her running group.
I cannot think of anything I would enjoy less.
I used to run. I used to actually enjoy running. I would struggle through the first couple miles, then zone out. My body knew what to do, and my mind could go wherever it wanted to. It was so peaceful, and I was always proud of myself when I finished.
But, run with a group of people who have all been running together?
I haven't run since Sarah was born. I would embarrass myself. They would all roll their eyes at me because I would either slow them down, pass out, or maybe even die. No, I'm sure

they wouldn't roll their eyes if I died, and Charlotte would not let anyone be mean to me, I am sure of it. She would probably say something encouraging, then everyone would smile, feel good and perfect Charlotte would fix everything. I am much more comfortable embarrassing myself in the comfort of my own home, thank you very much.

Chapter Twenty-Eight

Charlotte invited Samantha to her country club to play tennis. Samantha had not played in years, but she was a college athlete, so how bad could she be? She put on her cute running skirt that easily doubled as a tennis skirt since it had pockets in the little short tights under the skirt. She did not have a top to go with it, so she added a fitted Nike t-shirt. She was amazed when she saw that she still had her tennis shoes from before the move.

She grabbed her tennis racquet, filled up her bottle of water, and jumped in the car. When she arrived, she was blown away by the beauty of the club. She never got into golf, so she hadn't been to many golf courses, but just a single look, and she knew it was a luxurious place to spend your time. The front of the main building had beautiful pillars and gorgeous planters overflowing with seasonal annuals. A long porch stretched along the entire back of the building where gentlemen sat sipping iced tea, lemonade, or the occasional cocktail in rocking chairs, staring out at the 18th hole. Stuck in her admiration for such an incredible place, she didn't even see Charlotte walk up.

"Hey, girl!" she said from a few feet away.

"Wow, Charlotte, this place is so beautiful. Thank you for inviting me here."

"You can come here with me anytime. I have tons of guest passes, and I would be happy to pay for you to come even if I didn't. Maybe you can bring your family to have dinner with us some time." Charlotte offered as they headed over to the courts. "I am sorry I didn't invite you sooner. The kids and I were not feeling well last week. I think it was just a little bug. It only lasted forty-eight hours. They bounced back sooner than I did. I lost ten pounds. Can you believe it? Probably just water weight. Anyway, I have balls, but because of silly club rules, all players have to wear collared shirts." She rolled her eyes and opened the door to the pro shop. "Find something you like and just put it on my tab. I'll wait for you out on the center court."

Samantha was slightly overwhelmed by the selection in the pro shop. The sections were separated by sports: golf, tennis, swimming, and casual. She assumed casual meant you want to wear something *country-cluby* without having to do anything. She headed over to the tennis section where a teenager was stringing a tennis racquet. He glanced in her direction, then went back to work, probably assuming she would just ask if she actually needed something. Most of the women's tennis tops had the name of the country club on it. Would they even let her buy that? If she wore it, would it be like pretending to be a member when she wasn't? She found a cute, light pink top that was pretty neutral, had no writing on it, and she thought it would look nice with her skirt. Actually, the color would look great on Charlotte. Her skin tone made so many colors pop. She peered over the counter and out the window to center court and noticed that it was, in fact, the same shirt that Charlotte was wearing. No wonder it looked familiar! She went back to the rack, grabbed the light green one instead.

After buying and changing into the new shirt (which she actually needed anyway), the two women warmed up. It was all coming back for Samantha. She made great contact with the ball and placed her hits to land right on the baseline or by the doubles alley.

The first set went to a tiebreaker, which Charlotte won. They each quickly recovered with water and got the second set started. Samantha was pumped that she was holding her own against someone who played regularly. She really wanted to win the second set, knowing they would probably just call it a tie and not play a third set or a tiebreaker. Samantha went up 3-1 in the second set and was feeling great. Then, she double-faulted. Nothing aggravated her more than her own mistakes. If her opponent, in any sport or competition, made a good play, she could give credit where credit was due and just try harder. But, when like now, she lost the point because she hit two balls into the net, there was no excuse. She never recovered from her frustration and lost that game. The fun, friendly game of tennis turned into her own personal worth test. She put more and more pressure on herself to play the perfect ball, hit a winner, or just win. Period.

Samantha lost the second set 3-6. Charlotte had managed to win five games straight. In Samantha's mind, however, she lost the next five games straight. She had become so competitive that she managed to lose all by herself with faults, hitting the ball out of bounds, and going for a high-risk winner when she could've just hit the ball over the net and continued play. Charlotte could tell she was unhappy and tried to cheer her up by reminding her that she played all the time and Samantha was just getting back into it, but she didn't want to hear it.

She made an excuse to skip lunch with Charlotte, and as soon as she got in the car and began to pull out, tears fell. She started to sob. Why was she crying? It was just supposed to be a fun tennis match with a friend. Why does she always feel like she has to win? Why does everything need to be mistake-free? She pulled into the driveway, ran inside, took a two-minute shower, and crawled into bed to brood.

Chapter Twenty-Nine

Charlotte left the country club after talking with a few friends on her way out. She frequently played against competitive people and knew their anger or frustration after a loss had very little to do with the person they were playing against. By now, she had learned to just say "good game" and give them space. This was the first time she saw Samantha's competitive side, but she was just getting to know her after all.

Since Samantha changed her mind about going out to lunch after their match, Charlotte made a stop at the local organic grocery store to make herself a salad from their salad bar. After she boxed up her meal, she detoured to the fresh produce section to grab some veggies to snack on later. That was where she ran into Carrie Anne Watson.

Carrie Anne was a nice woman and a great person to have as a neighbor. She looked out for other people like she was in the running for an award. If someone was sick, she was the one who started the meal train. If you were late for after school pickup, she would happily grab your kids for you and feed them a nutritious snack. If she heard you were going to be out of town, she would check your mail, take your garbage and recycle out to the curb for pick up, as well as assure you that she would have an eye on your house the entire time you were gone. She stood at what couldn't be more than five feet tall, had a platinum blond, 1950's coiffed hairdo, and wouldn't shop anywhere but Macy's. What she lacked in size, she more than made up for in personality. Most conversations with Carrie Anne were one-sided, but Charlotte liked her anyway.

"Oh My Gosh, Charlotte, Hey!" she squealed

"Hi, Carrie Anne. How are you doing?"

"I'm great. I was just on my way to make my delivery to the food bank and thought I would stop here and pick up a few more essentials they often ask for. You certainly look cute. Were you just playing tennis?"

"I was playing with our new neighbor, Samantha. Have you two met yet?"

"I meant to stop by and introduce myself, but I spent all yesterday prepping a special dessert for the ladies at the nursing home up the street. I cannot possibly show up at Samantha's house to welcome her to the neighborhood, empty-handed, can I?" She stopped for maybe one second and continued. "No. You're right. I should stop by and say hello. I can bring her something in a couple days. It will have to be really good to make up for it. Maybe I can make her my brownie recipe and even stop by the gift shop and get her a custom platter or something as a housewarming. Great idea, Charlotte. Thanks so much. See you soon."

Before Charlotte even knew what was going on, Carrie Anne was gone. That was what she had come to expect from their conversations, though. Most of the time, Carrie Anne talked for both of them, but Charlotte loved the way she always got credit for any ideas that Carrie Anne came up with while talking. She giggled, grabbed some carrots and cucumbers, and headed to the checkout.

Chapter Thirty

Roger noticed Samantha's old tennis shoes by the door when he arrived home.

"Wow, did you actually go out and play tennis today?

"Charlotte and I played a match at her club," Samantha stated.

"I guess you lost because you look like you are pouting," Roger said with a smirk. "You are no spring chicken anymore. Just because you used to be an athlete doesn't make you one for your whole life. Prescott bragged about their snooty country club when we met, saying he would be pleased to sponsor us, as if I want to spend time with more people like him. I hope you didn't crash and burn too bad. I have a reputation to uphold in this community."

Roger stood there, with a chastising, half-smile awaiting an answer. Samantha simply dropped her head, feeling defeated once again, and went back to the bedroom.

Loser:

I am such a loser. I am embarrassed because:

- *I played so poorly at the end of our match*
- *I played poorly because I got too competitive*
- *I spazzed out in front of Charlotte when I lost some and people were watching from her tennis team, member or not, I will never be asked to play again, I'm sure*
- *My whole day was a disaster because I couldn't get over my behavior*
- *Roger knows me too well. He knew I lost, embarrassed myself, and was too competitive without me even having to say a word. He was equally disgusted by and entertained by my failure.*

Chapter Thirty-One

Feeling too embarrassed the following morning to call Charlotte and apologize, Samantha saw Junior and Sarah off to school, then sat on the couch and ate two bowls of Lucky Charms. She was still in the pajama pants she wore to bed, along with an oversized t-shirt. She was absent-mindedly watching a show about deep ocean animals and checking her phone at the same time browsing back and forth between social media and solitaire. She yawned, stretched, and noticed how bad she smelled. She showered after tennis the day before but must have forgotten deodorant.

The doorbell rang. Samantha was tempted to jump up and hide behind the couch, but she had a large glass front door, and the woman standing on the other side saw her sitting there sprawled out, cell phone in one hand and cereal bowl resting on her belly.

She answered the door, wearing no bra, no makeup, hair unbrushed, a little blood on her cheek from a picked zit she was messing with during her last game of solitaire, and a marshmallow rainbow on her chest.

The woman eyed her up and down then said, "You must be Samantha. I'm Carrie Anne Watson. I live a few houses past Charlotte. She has told me so much about you. Are you busy?" she paused, glancing again at the state Samantha was in then over her shoulder at her mess of a house. "I'd love to chat for a bit." she pushed.

Carrie Anne didn't really wait for a response but rather took Samantha's pause as an invitation. She walked past Samantha into the living room. The TV was still playing the deep ocean show, but it was on mute, which made it look more like a screensaver. One couch had an empty laundry basket sitting on it right next to a very large pile of unfolded clothes. Samantha's Spanx and underwear were right on top for Carrie Anne's viewing pleasure. The other couch, on which Samantha had been lounging when Carrie Anne showed up, was empty, but the pillows were not arranged nicely, and a blanket was just tossed in the corner. The coffee table was sprinkled with crumbs, had several empty water bottles and used cups on it, in addition to her now nearly empty cereal bowl. She directed Carrie Anne to the less-cluttered couch to take a seat before offering coffee, hoping that would keep her from following her to the kitchen.

Carrie Anne had already started talking before they sat down, so Samantha waited for a good time to get a word in to offer a drink or even excuse herself to put a bra on. She went on and on about the amazing love of her life, her husband, Bobby, who changed diapers, walked their two little dogs, and did the family laundry. She talked about her Junior League friends and about a girls' weekend she just got back from, with her sorority sisters from college. She talked about how she was remodeling her kitchen and that it was hard for a perfectionist like herself to be around such a mess most of the time. Samantha thought back to the good-old-days when she had the energy to be a perfectionist.

What people rarely understand is that being a perfectionist doesn't mean that person is perfect or keeps their life perfect all of the time. At least in Samantha's world, the farther from perfect her life is, the farther away from perfect she is, the more stress she feels. A low-stress environment for her is a clean house, organized rooms, closets and drawers, and of course, her color-coded calendar. Thanks to Carrie Anne and her visit this morning, she now had a perfect example of perfectionist high-stress.

Carrie Anne glanced at her watch mid-sentence and quickly stood up. She had somewhere she needed to be but told Samantha not to worry; she would be back, next time with brownies. She continued to talk as she walked towards the door. Samantha waved goodbye as she closed the door and did a double-take, and she noticed a small green marshmallow clover on the right side of Carrie Anne's butt.

Chapter Thirty-Two

Samantha woke early and more motivated than she had been in ages. The school volunteer coordinator had called a few days before letting her know that her background check came back clear, and she was scheduled to begin her volunteering. Her assignment was to read with a handful of fifth-grade kids each week, one-on-one.

She showered, dried, and curled her hair, found a dress that she thought would be acceptable (really just a nicer version of a sundress), and added a cardigan over it. She accessorized with cute wedges (not her usual flip flops), a long beaded necklace, matching earrings, and with the help of Vaseline, her wedding band, which hadn't been worn since her pregnancy with Sarah. It added stress to think about how she would get her wedding band off later, but fortunately, she was busy enough to keep that as just a fleeting thought.

She walked across the street with the kids and signed into the office like a pro. Maybe this volunteering thing would be good for her. She should mention it to Dr. Pager or whoever she recommends the next time she goes in for therapy. She had energy. She was actually wearing real clothes and was contributing to society.

She loved the teacher to whom she was assigned. Mrs. Berg was tall with short whitish-blond hair, and it was easy to see that she sincerely cared for the kids in her class. Samantha sat in the back of the room for close to ten minutes before Mrs. Berg was ready for her to pull the first student out of class. She looked around the room while the class was finishing up a group read. As the teacher read, the students stared at their own copy of the book upon their desk or laps with full attention, anticipating what came next. The room theme was camping, which Samantha thought was a bit juvenile for fifth graders, but the students seemed to love it. The seating arrangement was flexible, so kids were spread out all over the classroom. A few students were sitting at desks, one in a hammock, two on big, fluffy pillows in a tent, one standing at the window with her book balanced on the sill, and at least five were bouncing on yoga balls. The rest spread out on the floor, rug, or on crates. Cute little camping lanterns were hung around the ceiling of the room, and in the corner stood a real, metal fire pit filled with books (to read, not to burn). The short thunderstorm that was passing through only added to the ambiance. Samantha envied these kids as she thought of how fun it would be to spend the day with Mrs. Berg.

She met with each of the four kids individually at a desk in a small break-out room. While she was meeting with the first student, a girl named Annie, her phone buzzed in her pocket. Samantha quickly reached into her pocket, silencing it, hoping Annie would not tell on her. Less than a minute later, it buzzed again. She silenced it again, feeling even more like a rule breaker. As she walked Annie back to class, she felt a different buzz on her hip. She had a text message. She covertly pulled her phone out and saw that it was Roger.

Why won't you answer my calls?
Did you decline my call twice?
What could you possibly be doing that is so important?

Samantha wrote a quick message back.

At school. Volunteering. Be home later.

She opened the door for Annie, called out the next student, and walked back to the small room. After working with them just once, she realized that the first three were only slightly behind but could use the extra reading time for practice. But the last child she met with had so much trouble she wondered how he managed to get past second grade. She held one copy of the passage he was reading, and he held another. To see an improvement in his reading speed, she was instructed have him read the passage multiple times whilst timing it. On the first attempt, she paid close attention to the paper as he stumbled on every sentence. The second time, he made almost every mistake again, in the exact same places. The third time, she practically had the script memorized, so she watched him as he read. She noted that his hair was greasy with considerable dandruff. His shoes were taped up with duct tape. His hands shook slightly as he held the paper, and she hoped she wasn't making him uncomfortable. She took a deep breath and empathized with his struggle. She had found it difficult reading out loud as a child. She remembered how she would get sick to her stomach when called on by the teacher. The more nervous she became, the harder it was for her to concentrate on the words. Samantha noticed she started to sweat, receiving an elevated heart rate alert from her watch right after. In the middle of his last passage, she excused herself to the ladies' room to splash some water on her face. How could she save him the humiliation she went through as a child? How could she help him gain the confidence he needed to succeed in reading and life? He was so sweet and likely had some sort of undiagnosed learning disability, but she committed to making a difference in his reading before middle school.

When she returned to the break-out room, the boy was gone, but there was a note in his place.

Mrs. Berg came and got me for lunch. Thanks for helping me. Steven

Tears flooded her eyes, but she couldn't let anyone see her like this. After about ten minutes, Samantha regained her composure and then walked up to the front office to check out.

She thought about Steven throughout the day and wondered what his home life was like. Teachers have huge classes full of kids with all different types of problems, obstacles, baggage... how does Mrs. Berg go home every night and detach from her worries about her students when Samantha knew she wouldn't be able to get this boy off her mind.

When she arrived back at home, she kept up her productivity momentum throughout the day by making notes on her calendar, writing up a grocery list, cleaning the toilets, and making herself a healthy sandwich and small cup of tomato soup. From dumpy pajamas and cereal to classy dresses and soup, she knew it was a good change.

She could not wait to brag to the kids about her productive day, but she saw that Sarah was crying when they walked in. Sweet Junior looked concerned but clueless. Samantha sent Junior away to the office to work on his homework, and she pulled Sarah aside to talk. While she waited for Sarah's breathing to slow, she grabbed an ice pop out of the freezer. She knew she would have to give one to Junior eventually, but this was her way to settle them down and get them ready to talk.

Sarah explained between hitched breaths that she was in big trouble because of something that happened at school. Samantha waited patiently for her to continue. When she finally recovered, she started to explain.

"I was playing during my free time with the dollhouse in our classroom. One of the boys in our class complained to the teacher that he didn't have anything to do, so she sent him to play with me since I was the only one at the dollhouse. He is really rough and not nice with the dolls or their things. He likes to put all of the dolls into the bed together, and when no-one is looking, he switches their heads or just takes the heads off and puts them in the oven or under the blankets of the bed. He knows it bothers me when he mixes up the rooms, so he started taking all of the furniture, dishes, and everything else out of the kitchen and put it in the bathroom. The bathroom was so crowded that the 'frigerator, that was now sitting next to the potty, opened, and the milk and cheese and chicken all fell out onto the floor. I said he was making an 'f word' mess, and he ran to tell the teacher on me." Sarah began to cry again.

After sucking some more on her ice pop, she tried to finish. "Mrs. Parsley took me to the principal's office, but they made me wait in the hall while they talked. When she came out, she told me that you need to come to talk to her and Mr. Small before school tomorrow."

Samantha pulled her into a hug and asked where she heard that word.

"I hear it on cartoons all the time. Junior and dad say it. I thought everyone said it."

Roger often steps outside to take work calls. He thinks that gives him privacy, but he talks so loud it's as if he is talking into a tin can be connected by a string to another tin can in the next room. Anyone within earshot can tell by his calls that he is a totally different person at work than he is at home. He seems so entertaining on the phone, outgoing and jovial, and curses a lot.

He has always been very proper around the kids. Junior and Sarah have said *please, thank you, yes ma'am,* and *no sir* since birth. He would never say a curse word in front of the kids or even Samantha because, of course, she's a lady. But listen to him talk on the phone when he ducks outside for a call, and phrases like 'shit storm' and 'for fucks sake' flow naturally out of his mouth.

Samantha made a mental note to check on what Sarah was watching on TV and speak with Roger about his language. But, when Roger arrived home, she decided it was best to not bring it up. He would either A) get really mad at Samantha because everything that goes wrong is her fault or B) get so mad at Sarah that Samantha would have to step in, and that would make him even angrier. Sarah certainly wouldn't bring it up with Roger, and Junior never really understood what happened. If it turned out to be a big problem, she would talk to him after the meeting tomorrow.

She fell asleep, pondering how an interaction would be between Mr. Small and Roger. They would either hit it off like long-lost brothers or tear each other to shreds. She was beginning to realize that if they ever got together, she hoped for the latter.

Monday:

I can't sleep thinking about this meeting tomorrow. There is nothing I can do about it now, so I am trying to get my mind off it. I have been scrolling through Facebook, and my emotions range from envy to aggravation.

- *Jonathan from high school, who was an average soccer player, was recruited his senior year to kick for the football team, and now he is a starter for an NFL team*
- *Debbie from college married a movie star she met at a wedding in Spain and now lives in one of her three mansions*
- *Tiffany, from her old job, who was one of those people who are smart and pretty and nice and you wonder how you fit it all in one package, has four beautiful daughters, who are all modeling in NYC*

- My own mom posts photos of her creations from her art class, which would sell out at the most exclusive of galleries

Why does it seem that good fortune falls into the laps of everyone else? Where is my talent? Where is my golden ticket? Do any of these people get in fights with their spouses? Have they ever been sick? I guess I will never know because none of them post anything but what they want the world to see. Then we can continue to hold them up on a pedestal and feel jealous of them and worse about our own lives.

As I thought about my shit life, I thought of one of the boys I read with at school. His name is Steven Glenn, so I thought I would see if I could find his family on Facebook? Is that ethical? I felt weird doing it, but I am only looking because I worry about him. I found one woman within twenty miles with the same last name, so I clicked on her profile and immediately knew I found the right person. Tabitha Glenn lives about three miles from us in a mobile home park with her five children. The pictures are all of her and the kids, and her status was single. She had two jobs listed: a stock person at Target and one on the night cleaning crew at a local business park. She looked young but aged by overwork, heartbreak, and many kids, but she had a nice smile in every picture and always held her kids tight. Her life is likely not easy, but it made me feel better to know that Steven has someone at home who loves him.

Chapter Thirty-Three

Samantha planned to wake early and go through her new routine again, but after not sleeping much the night before worrying about the meeting with Mr. Small this morning, she didn't feel as energetic. She dressed in her only other appropriate outfit, ate a banana, so she didn't pass out, and walked with her kids to school.

When the receptionist saw her check-in, she asked Sarah to sit in the front office and wait, then she directed Samantha to Mr. Small's office. Samantha felt like all eyes were on her. The receptionist, who was so kind just yesterday, looked disappointed in her. Did she know what happened? Did the whole staff know what happened? Did all the parents in the class already know? Was this how her family would be known at this school, the bad parents who taught their hoodlum kids bad words? What if someone at the school knows Roger or knows someone who works in his office. What if this whole thing gets back to him before she tells him. Oh, he would be so mad... the embarrassment of hearing something bad about his own daughter from someone other than his wife. She shuddered to think of it.

Mr. Small's office was the size of at least two classrooms. She got the strong whiff of cologne when she walked through the door, almost as if he used it as an air freshener or was trying to desperately cover up some other smell. The furniture was all dark wood and leather, and his library on the wall was extensive. The office seemed a better fit for a smoking club or defense attorney than a principal at an elementary school. He had pictures everywhere of himself standing with the school board members as if they were famous celebrities. He also had American flags everywhere like a politician.

He glared at her as she walked in and directed her to the chair across the desk from him. He began by rehashing the same story that Sarah had told her but without a girl's sweet innocent voice, very serious about her doll play. He kept his voice down, but his tone was abrasive. Samantha attempted to speak, but he immediately shut her down, talking about how a situation like this can damage a child's reputation, especially one that is new to the school. Then, he went on to talk about the poor boy whose ears had to hear that awful word. He went on to ask if the adults in the house speak like that in front of the kids, and it hit her. Mr. Small sounds just like Roger. When Roger is angry, he talks to her in the same rude, condescending way. He had completely dismissed her and clearly didn't care about Sarah's side or what Samantha had to say. He only wanted to put her in her place and move on.

Just then, Charlotte popped her head in. She looked amazing and was somehow confident enough to just pop into the principal's office.

"Is everything okay in here, Mr. Small? I believe we have our weekly meeting this morning," she said in the most professional tone while eyeing me in a concerned way. Charlotte is the PTA president and has been very involved in the school since her oldest, the same age as Junior, was in Kindergarten.

"Good morning, Mrs. Callahan," he said in a very sing-song voice quite unlike the one he was using with Samantha. "We are finishing up here. I'll just be a minute more."

Charlotte looked back and forth between Mr. Small and Samantha, gasped, and said, "Is everything okay? Are the kids okay?"

Mr. Small smiled and opened his mouth to say something, but Samantha jumped in. "Sarah said the 'f-word' in class yesterday."

"That doesn't sound like her." Charlotte scoffed at the two of them. "Did she tell you that?"

"She told me the whole story yesterday. Something happened while she was playing with a classmate at the dollhouse station, and she blurted out that he made an 'f-ing mess.' All of this is odd because I didn't even know she knew that word. She said she hears it all the time." Samantha buried her head in her hands.

"Did you, by chance, ask her what the f-word was?" Charlotte asked.

Mr. Small answered in a challenging yet respectful voice, "Mrs. Callahan, we don't want this child to say the word and do more damage than she has already done."

Samantha bristled, hearing him refer to Sarah so impersonally.

Charlotte turned on her heel and left the room. Samantha stared in awe. She couldn't get a word in edgewise, and Mr. Small let Charlotte go on and on and actually listened to her. Samantha thought that she should consider the PTA.

Less than a minute later, Charlotte returned with Sarah.

Charlotte knelt down in front of her and asked, "Sarah, can you please tell us exactly what you said to the little boy in your class yesterday? Don't worry. You will not get in trouble if you say it just this time."

Sarah looked at Samantha, then looked to Mr. Small, waiting for a sign that it was okay. Sarah nodded, then Mr. Small followed suit.

"He messed up the kitchen. All of the food fell out of the 'frigerator, so I told him he was making a freaking mess."

Charlotte gave Sarah a big against-the-rules hug, thanked her, and walked her back to the front office. A smile grew slowly across Samantha's face. She thought she might giggle uncontrollably the way you might at a funeral or other times when it is completely inappropriate. Mr. Small sat with his mouth agape, trying to compose himself. He mumbled a few things about misunderstanding and thanked her for coming in.

Samantha stood up, walked out to the office, then out the front door without even checking out, like a rock star.

<u>Tuesday:</u>

I love my kids, but I know they are not perfect. It always bothers me when moms don't think their kids could possibly ever do anything wrong. They deny any accusations up and down even when they are staring the problem right in the face. I always intend to support my kids, but sadly, if someone accuses my kids of something, I normally believe them. Why would another mom lie? Why would another mom make it up? There have been times when Kid A tells Mom A that Kid B did something bad. Mom A complains to Mom B. If I am Mom B, I want to know. I would want to know that my kid is acting up, bullying, or in this case, cursing, rather than people try to keep it from me and talk about my kids behind my back. I would accuse my Kid B but still, listen to their side of the story. More times than not, Kid A was a little liar, and I feel horrible for not believing my kids from the start. I guess it is just that I know my kids' poop stinks just like everyone else's does.

Chapter Thirty-Four

Samantha invited Charlotte to lunch as both a thank you for handling Mr. Small and an apology for tennis, neither of which she actually stated. They decided on a quaint farm-to-table restaurant on the river. They were lucky to get a nice table by the window and talked about anything but their lives, like storms in the Caribbean, Charlotte's amazing shoe collection, and which actress is dating which rock star.

After receiving their meals, Charlotte invited Samantha (and Roger) to meet her, Prescott, and a few other couples for trivia night at a bar about a quarter mile from their house. Samantha normally uses the easy, mostly true excuse that although she and Roger would love to, he will be at work late. But today, she was in a particularly good mood, so she agreed that they would at least try to make it there.

Unexpectedly, Roger waltzed in with his work buddies, loud and obnoxious like a bunch of frat boys. After a few minutes of visible and loud disturbances, he saw the ladies looking at his group from where they were sitting in the corner. He quickly excused himself from his friends and walked over to their table as a completely different man.

"Well, hello, ladies. This is an unexpected surprise. Please pardon my associates. They can be a bit loud," he said as he grabbed onto Samantha's shoulders from behind her chair.

Charlotte stood and gave him a hug, "It's so great to see you, Roger. I was just telling Samantha that we are meeting some friends out for trivia night tomorrow evening, and I was really hoping you two could make it. I know you have to work late, but…"

"Nonsense," he interrupted. "We would love to meet you. It's not as if I can't take off whenever I want." he chuckled. "I am pretty high up the chain of command," he said with a wink. "We will see you there."

He bent over, kissed Samantha on the top of the head, and gave Charlotte an awkward wave as he rejoined his group at their table.

When the ladies finished their lunch and were heading out, Samantha overheard one of the guys with Roger ask, "Who is that fine piece of ass with your wife?"

Samantha turned quickly, very surprised and disgusted, but none of the men looked up.

"My wife's new, best friend. I can't wait until she comes over to our pool this summer!" Roger said in the most piggish way possible, cupping his hands in front of his chest. The whole table laughed.

Horrified, Samantha quickly gave Charlotte an air-kiss and jumped in her car, wondering if it was at all possible that Charlotte didn't hear the interaction. She had never heard him speak that way except on the phone. How can he be two totally different people?

Samantha thought back to when she met Roger on her drive home, searching for signs that she must have missed that he had this other side. They first met at a bar, where they were both out with friends. There was such an instant attraction that they spent the whole evening in a corner booth, just the two of them. They were inseparable at the beginning of their courtship except, of course, when they both were at work. He spent nearly every night at her apartment and would only run home for new clothes and a shower. The only time he ever showed signs of being anything but the sweet, doting boyfriend she was falling in love with was once when he clogged the toilet at her place and yelled at her for asking if she could help or at least pass him a plunger.

As she thought back, she recalled that they never went out with friends. It was always just the two of them. She had suggested they go on double dates before, but his answers always pointed towards him wanting to spend more time with just her, rather than him not wanting to socialize with other people. In fact, he never went out with friends, never talked about friends, or was invited to anything that she knew of.

When she wanted to go to an event like a wedding or party, rather than telling her not to, like he does now, he would tell her he had something special planned and would whisk her away on a spontaneous getaway. It was very exciting, but as she thought back, it did seem like he kept her away from people, in addition to the fact that she never really saw what he was like around others. For their own wedding, she had always dreamed of a big wedding with relatives and friends from all over. All Roger wanted was to go to an island, grab some lifeguard to be our witness, and get married under the sun in private. So that is what they did. The way he proposed the idea was so romantic, but she still to this day yearns for the wedding she never had. She thought back to lunch earlier that day and the fact that he did not introduce her to even one of his many coworkers that were with him. He didn't seem angry that she was out with Charlotte, but he is a very good actor, and she may see his true colors in the evening.

Chapter Thirty-Five

Samantha and Sarah sat in the auditorium's third row, waiting to watch Junior's school play. They had arrived twenty minutes early to get a good seat, and ever since they sat down, Samantha had been texting Roger's phone in hopes that he may make it in time, or at all. She was saving one more chair for Roger and was getting worried that he wouldn't show. At least five people had asked if that seat was saved, and she would look like a real ass if the show started, and no one was sitting there, but she couldn't even imagine the backlash if Roger walked in at the last minute and there was no seat for him. The least he could do was text her back to let her know if he had intentions of coming or not.

The principal stood up in front of the crowd to introduce the play, and the crowd got quiet. Samantha gave one last look to the rear of the auditorium in hopes Roger had miraculously appeared. Instead, a woman a few rows behind her, staring patiently at the stage wearing a huge smile on her face, caught her eye. Then she saw one of the four kids with her was Steven from her reading group. She remembered him telling her that he had a sister in the same grade as Junior. So this woman, a single mom, who works at least two jobs, managed to get here with her four other kids in tow to watch her daughter perform. But, not Roger. Samantha turned in her seat to face forward as she heard the announcements wrapping up.

When Mr. Small was finished talking, he walked over to Samantha and asked if he could sit in the open seat. She was grateful that he would be sitting there knowing the play was now starting, even if in the slim chance that Roger actually showed up, he would just stand at the back rather than walk up to our row in front of everyone.

The play was as normal school plays are. Some of the lines cannot be heard, some parts are horribly boring, some fun songs, and some parts are hilarious but normally for all of the wrong reasons. About twenty kids had speaking parts and at least sixty more stood on risers in the background and joined in for the songs. Junior only had two lines, probably the least out of the speaking parts, but his two lines were the comic relief of the play, and he hammed it up. First, he said, "What do you think I am, a typewriter?" and everyone laughed so hard the next three lines by other actors were completely missed. A bit later, he said, "If you say so." and people were doubled over in their chairs. His delivery was amazing, and he totally stole the show with those two little lines. Samantha's favorite part was watching Sarah's look of pride as Junior crossed the stage and delivered his lines. She would watch him, and then when he was done with his line, she looked around the audience to see the reaction. She was so proud of her big brother.

When the play ended, and everyone was collecting their kids and heading out to their cars, Samantha bumped into Charlotte and Leslie.

"Girl! Junior was a riot! I am so glad he got that part instead of that pompous ass, Chester." started Leslie.

"Leslie! He is just a kid," whispered Charlotte.

"Oh, I know. But he has tried to take over every play since Kindergarten, and he wasn't even funny." Leslie continued, "Is Roger out of town? I didn't see him here tonight."

"No, he is in town but must have gotten stuck at work," Samantha explained.

"Too bad for him. Or maybe it is good in the long run. Not all dads are comfortable with their kids being thespians." Leslie laughed at herself just as all of the kids ran over.

They all walked out together, and random people would stop to congratulate Junior. Samantha checked her phone again to see if Roger texted to let her know where he was or even see how Junior performed. Nothing.

When Samantha, Junior, and Sarah arrived home, Roger's car was in the driveway. As soon as Junior and Sarah walked into the house, they ran excitedly up to Roger, who was sitting on the couch, eating a sandwich and watching the news. Samantha couldn't believe he was home and never answered her, but the kids were so excited to tell him about the play that she didn't want to spoil the mood.

<u>Wednesday:</u>

I am disappointed that Roger didn't make an effort to make it to Junior's play tonight. Actually, I am confused. I just don't understand, but I don't dare ask or confront him. I am excited to go out with Roger to meet up with friends for trivia night tomorrow. I don't know if we've ever gone out with other couples like this. If we had, I have forgotten. I was hoping to talk about it tonight, at least to be sure he will actually go through with it and not bail, but Roger was very cold to me when we arrived home. He was not mean. I guess I would describe it as indifference. He just didn't seem to care that I was there. He listened attentively as Junior and Sarah told him about the play, and he looked happy and proud, but if I added anything in, it was as if he didn't hear it. He did not bring up lunch or the fact that I was out with Charlotte.

I didn't bring up the play or the fact that he didn't introduce any of his coworkers to me at lunch. I'm pretty sure he doesn't know that I overheard his crass conversation about Charlotte, but I wouldn't know because he didn't want anything to do with me. It's as if he was exhausted from pretending to be a nice guy all day and can't fake it anymore when he gets home. Maybe it is from Roger that Junior gets his acting skills. When I left the living room to go to bed, I kissed him on the head and said goodnight. His response was just, "Tomorrow is going to suck for me. I hope you know that."

Chapter Thirty-Six

Samantha received a text from Charlotte the next day to let her know that trivia night started at seven, so she spent the afternoon scheduling a babysitter and trying to find something to wear that would be attractive but not too attractive. What would Roger like to see me in? What outfit would make him proud to show me off but not attract too much attention?

She finally settled on a tight pair of jeans looking only slightly worn just above one knee and a light peach, chiffon shirt. You could see her black lace bra through the shirt, but it looked more classy than slutty. She threw on some small diamond stud earrings and a dainty gold chain with a small bar that said LOVE on it, then topped it all off with the pair of sexy Jimmy Choo stilettos that Charlotte loaned her.

By 6:45, the babysitter had arrived and took the kids upstairs to watch a movie in the playroom. While Samantha nervously waited for Roger to get home, she poured a glass of Pinot Noir. She debated whether to give him a call to be sure he was on the way, but just took another sip instead. Glass in hand, she wandered over to the door to look for his car. Just as she peeked out the window, he pulled up.

"What? Are you waiting for me at the door?" he snapped. "Are you drinking already? What the heck, Samantha? You can't wait ten more minutes until we get to the bar? Are you even allowed to drink on all your crazy-lady meds?"

Samantha stood there, shocked and speechless, but it didn't matter; Roger had already walked into the bedroom to change. She wandered into the kitchen, not feeling nearly as confident as she had just a few minutes earlier. She poured the wine down the drain, washed the glass, and took a seat on a barstool at the counter.

"Well, are we going or not?" Roger said as he strutted into the room.

Samantha followed him out to the car in the garage and hopped in his passenger seat. He started the car and, as he was backing out, muttered, "Nice bra, let's show your tits to the whole neighborhood, why don't we?"

Chapter Thirty-Seven

Samantha and Roger walked into Ziggy's, a little neighborhood dive bar, just as the first round of trivia was getting ready to start. Charlotte ran over, handed them their trivia answer cards (which were just index cards with a sticker on the back that said "Ziggy's Trivia Night"), and pulled Samantha by the hand to their table. She introduced the first-timers to everyone else, but it was obvious Roger either wasn't listening or, more likely, just didn't care. Probably both. He was checking to see who needed a drink and headed off to the bar.

The bar was dark as bars often are. Large, glass bulb lights lined the exposed rustic, wooden beams that crossed the ceiling but were clearly more for decoration than lighting. A large bar made out of old surfboards lined one entire side of the room. Television screens hung on the wall behind the bar, all showing different surfing competitions. Either the TVs were on mute, or the loud music playing drowned out whatever was on there. A small stage stood at one end of the room where the trivia night people stood, getting ready to begin. The music volume dropped slightly as the MC announced the first question.

Name the 1973 movie featuring the song, 'Time Warp.'

Charlotte put an arm around Samantha and said, "Hey, you're actually here! Relax, have fun, answer some questions, and win us a pitcher of beer." She let her arm drop, grabbed her drink, and took a sip. She giggled to herself then nudged Samantha in the arm. "Look at Prescott," she said, still sounding giddy. "He is taking this so seriously. He already has his name on his card, numbered the lines for his answers, and has secluded himself so no one will steal his answers. I am not sure he realized the rest of us are not even writing anything down."

Samantha looked over to Prescott. He did look like he was in game mode. She envied the way Charlotte looked at Prescott and his dorky game obsession with a smile. She knew it was strange and that even though no one else in the whole bar was taking it that seriously, she thought it was cute. She wondered how someone can take their partner's goofy flaws and turn them into adorable quirks.

Name the musical group with the album titled, 'Licensed to Ill.'

"Relax, girl. Have fun," Charlotte said again.

Until she mentioned it, Samantha had not noticed how uptight she was feeling. She forced a smile to show Charlotte, she was happy to be there, just as Roger was on his way back from the bar. He held three pitchers of beer in each hand and was being followed by the 5'10, gorgeous bartender holding a tray of a dozen full shot glasses. Samantha had not taken shots in years and was happy to see that the shots were not straight liquor but mixed shooters. They were bigger than the average shot but mixed with something else.

How many members are in Maroon 5?

He set the beer on the table and handed out the shots to the group. He held up his glass and said, "To beautiful women!" tipped back his shot, slammed the glass on the table and grabbed Charlotte, and landed a huge kiss right on her mouth. It's hard to say whether he was going for her cheek and he just missed, or that was his intention, but he certainly didn't pull away. Samantha just stared in horror, then quickly looked around for Prescott, who was asking the trivia game leaders a question on the other side of the bar.

Which chess piece can only move diagonally?

Roger let go of Charlotte, then proceeded to kiss every woman at the table. One husband finally objected, so he planted a big smacker on him too, and everyone laughed. "More shots!" he yelled on his way back to the bar.

Where would you find the Sea of Tranquility?

"Wow, your husband is a riot." said one of the men at the table. The trivia game continued, Roger continued to drink, getting rowdier and rowdier.

Which word goes before bikini, beans, and quartet?

This was another side of Roger she was not used to seeing. Samantha would be talking to Charlotte and happen to glance around and see Roger just staring, no shame, right at Charlotte's chest. Thankfully, neither Charlotte nor Prescott seemed to notice. You would've thought the prize for winning the trivia game was for a new car or boat the way Prescott was taking it so seriously.

Name the seventh planet from the sun.

A couple hours later, Roger put his arm around Samantha, stared right into Charlotte's cleavage, then up to her eyes, and said, "Charlotte, I am so glad you invited us. We should do this more often. But, sadly, we have to go. The babysitter can't stay out too late."

What is the actress's name that plays the protagonist in the movie
"Sleeping with the Enemy"?

Samantha gave Charlotte a big hug and headed towards the door. Samantha noticed Roger hugged her too, but maybe a little longer than normal.

Name the only heavyweight boxing champion to finish his career
of forty-nine fights without ever having been defeated?

The door to the bar had not even shut, and old Roger was back. "What the heck, Samantha? What do you tell these people about me? They all think I am some uptight workaholic."

"I don't say anything about you. They just notice we don't join everyone in neighborhood activities."

"So, why is it then that they don't assume you are the uptight one? Is it because your bra is showing and you are wearing super-high, stripper heels like a whore?"

Samantha didn't get a chance to answer. Roger had already sat down in his car, closed the door, and started the engine.

"Maybe I should drive," Samantha said in a timid voice as she slid in the passenger seat, knowing he would never allow her to do it.

"Maybe I should start trusting women with financial decisions or the government, too." he laughed and pulled out so fast that surely a skid mark was left behind.

Thursday Night:

Things that made me Happy tonight:

- *Roger and I actually went out with friends.*
- *We stayed longer than I expected.*
- *I felt pretty good in my outfit... for a while.*
- *I was able to meet some new people.*
- *I am pretty sure I got every trivia question right.*
- *That redhead at the bar said Roger is a good kisser*
- *Beth said the kids were well behaved while we were out*
- *Leslie said Beth is thinking of moving to the area. How awesome would that be to have her as a regular babysitter?*

Things that made me Sad tonight:

- *I forgot the names of everyone we met this evening*
- *I may have stretched Charlotte's nice shoes she lent me. They were tight, then they were not.*
- *Roger made me feel like my outfit was ugly and I am unattractive*
- *Roger kissed at least four other women and two men, and somehow he was the life of the party*
- *I am not sure who this man is who I married*
- *That redhead at the bar was a man*
- *I never want to go out with friends again*

Chapter Thirty-Eight

When the trivia competition ended, Charlotte tipped and thanked their waitress, said her goodbyes, and made her way out to the car. Prescott, of course, won trivia night again. He won the monthly competition for the last three months. She thought the bar owners would be angry, but to watch how serious he was about it when the other patrons tuned out made them happy. Not to mention, the excitement he generated when he won was contagious. Charlotte slipped into the driver's seat, started the car, and turned on the radio to a classical station at a low volume. She didn't want to dull Prescott's celebration, but she was done; done with the sticky floors, done with the belligerent drunks, done with the loud music. She didn't mind waiting. In fact, she was happier waiting in the car. Around ten minutes later, Prescott emerged, looking like a kid that just won his first trophy. He practically skipped to the car holding his coupons for a free pitcher of beer in one hand and a #1 foam finger in the other. He climbed into the car and looked at her proudly. She couldn't help but smile. She was not a big fan of bars, but she would do anything to see him this happy.

As they drove home, he gave a play-by-play of the entire evening of trivia and repeated over and over that he couldn't believe he had been able to win by so much with such easy questions.

Charlotte dropped Prescott off in front of the house and drove the babysitter home. When she returned, she walked into the living room to find Prescott wearing nothing but his foam finger. His trophy placement was better than their headboard, which is where he had become accustomed to displaying them. She laughed out loud at his new interesting placement, then followed him into the bedroom.

Chapter Thirty-Nine

Some days, having a commitment of some sort is the only thing that gets Samantha out of the house. Just days after the trivia night, the speed of her depression slide was getting faster and faster. She pictured herself on one of those old, long metal slides from the '80s that would burn your skin, and Roger standing next to the slide pouring oil on it with an evil smile on his face.

Fortunately, she agreed to help Carrie Anne at the PTA Christmas Tree lot today, or she would've just stayed in bed all day. If it were anyone else, she would have canceled, but she was a bit intimidated by Carrie Anne and didn't want to feel guilty all day for bailing.

It was a chilly morning, so she dressed in jeans and a fitted sweater. The sweater was not likely meant to be fitted, but her stomach was nearing the size of someone who was six months pregnant. She threw a puffy vest over it, pulled her hair back, and walked to school.

The crisp, cool air was actually refreshing, so she started to get excited. She pictured herself in the cute, little shack they had in the tree lot, listening to Christmas music and sipping hot cocoa next to the floor heater. Carrie Anne greeted her at the fence, next to a big sign that said PTA Winter Tree Sale.

"Winter Tree Sale?" Samantha asked.

"Oh, you know, we don't want to offend anyone who doesn't celebrate Christmas," she explained.

"Do people who don't celebrate Christmas buy Winter Trees?"

"It doesn't matter. Follow me." Carrie Anne said abruptly and turned towards the shack. "I will be in the Winter Shack and will take payment from anyone ready to buy. Oh, I forgot to mention. Since you are volunteering, you get a 10% discount when you buy your tree." she said way more excitedly than the actual statement warranted.

"Thanks, but we have an artificial tree," Samantha said plainly.

Carrie Anne audibly gasped and covered her mouth with her hand. It was as if what Samantha said were so appalling and unheard of that she couldn't believe it could be true and especially couldn't believe she would admit to such an atrocity out loud.

Samantha loved her artificial tree. There were no needles to clean up, no water to fill, no squirrels to jump out at you while you are putting up lights, no disposal... just put it up, take it down, store it until next year. I was even pre-lit. She was not the slightest bit ashamed, but the look on Carrie Anne's face made her feel as if she should be.

Carrie Anne abruptly turned to walk away, saying, "You are to walk the lot and answer any questions people have, or point them to me if they are ready to buy."

Samantha looked around at the lot, which was about the same size as a tractor-trailer, with about ten trees standing and the rest behind the shack. Was she supposed to walk around these ten trees for her entire four-hour shift? As she watched Carrie Anne walk back into the shack, she wondered why they both needed to be there. It was 9am, people were at work, and kids were in school. Who was out buying their "Winter Tree" at this time of day?

She shook off the thought and tried to get herself pumped up for a nice morning of retail. She had always wanted to work in a store. As a kid, she played 'grocery store' with her friends all of the time. She would be the one to straighten the food on the shelves and sort the money while everyone else would fill carts and dump them at the register. She had hoped she would be the one to run the checkout, but clearly, she had not risen that high on the Winter Tree Sales ladder yet.

She closed her eyes and listened to the music playing. Brittney Spears was not what she thought she would be listening to while selling Christmas Trees, but it was something. She walked around the trees, feeling each of them, seeing if they were stable, well-watered, not dropping needles, but when she was done, only ten minutes had passed. There were no cars in the visitor's lot, and no one was approaching, so she pulled her book out of her purse to read. She may not be invited to sit in the cozy shack, but she could sit by a tree and enjoy her book. After reading the first sentence, her phone pinged. She pulled out her phone to read the incoming text message.

Hey Girl. No reading while you're on the clock ;)

Samantha rolled her eyes, placed her phone and book back in her purse, and got back to pacing the lot.

Nearly four hours passed, and not one customer came to the lot. During the last hour, her sole entertainment was when she could see some kids at a distance on the playground. Just as she was preparing to head home at the end of her shift, Samantha saw a well-dressed, middle-aged man approach. He walked into the lot and started browsing trees. Samantha was so excited for her first, and most likely, only customer, that she immediately approached him and said, "Good morning, is there anything, in particular, you are looking for?"

"Yeah. A tree," he replied in a rude and condescending tone.

She stood speechless. She was so embarrassed. She had been getting ready for this moment all day, and that was the question she asked? Maybe that was the kind of question one would ask when working at a department store with thousands of items, but a tree lot?

The man sighed loudly, turned his back to Samantha, and walked away. Her embarrassment turned to anger. How could that man be so rude, especially at Christmastime? She was volunteering for a school, for crying out loud! As she watched him walk away, she recognized that arrogant strut, that demeanor that cares for no-one, that attitude that he was better than her and she was not worthy of talking to him... he was just like Roger.

"What happened? Did you scare off our first customer?" Carrie Anne asked, only partially kidding.

"I think my shift is over. I am heading home, Carrie Anne." Samantha said dejectedly as she started to walk towards the gate.

"Okay, well, thanks for your help. I hope you had fun!" Carrie Anne called after her.

Fun would be if she had driven and could 'accidentally' run over that asshole with her car. It was probably for the best that she walked.

Chapter Forty

Christmas had always been Samantha's favorite holiday. She loved the build-up, the shopping, the decorations, the music, the treats, but nothing was as much fun to her as seeing the joy on Junior and Sarah's faces on Christmas morning.

She had not been in the mood to get dressed up and go shopping, so she did almost all of her gift buying online from her bedroom. Though it was not the same, she still enjoyed getting the gifts hidden when they arrived, keeping notes of what she had already purchased and for whom. She would occasionally get out of bed to wrap presents, but she liked to keep them hidden until Christmas Eve, so Christmas morning was even more magical.

The kids have been out of school for a few days now leading up to the big day, so she made sure to have everything completed last week. She had tried multiple times to talk with Roger about gifts for the kids, but he seemed to be pushing her away even more than normal.

She reminisced about what Christmas Eve was like for her and Roger when they were first married. They lit a fire in the fireplace, turned on a Christmas movie, ate popcorn, and sipped hot chocolate.

She thought she would surprise him this Christmas Eve and rekindle their tradition.

When Christmas Eve arrived, and the kids were snuggled in bed, she walked out to the family room where Roger was sitting with hot chocolate and popcorn. A Christmas movie was playing, but it was on mute, and Roger was playing Bubble Mania on his phone. She put the popcorn on the coffee table, sat next to him, and handed him his mug.

He raised his hand without looking up and simply said, "No, thanks."

She sat in silence, hoping when he finished, he would pick it up, drink it, put an arm around her, turn the volume back up on the TV... anything. But, as soon as his game was over, he opened another app to watch funny videos.

"Do you not want your hot chocolate?" she said timidly.

"Why are you pushing hot chocolate on me? What did you do, lace it with Arsenic?" he said with a laugh.

"I am going to get all the presents out of the closet. Do you want to come?"

"No, thanks," he said, still staring at his phone.

She realized she should have asked for help rather than asking if he wanted to participate. She had so many presents to bring out, some of them heavy, not to mention six boxes of the parts that needed assembling for Junior's new drum kit. She was past trying to include him, she just wanted help.

She stood abruptly and sighed as she walked back to her room. Samantha spent the next four hours assembling the drum kit and daydreaming about spiking Roger's coffee.

As exhausted as Samantha was after toting every present out to the living room, perfectly arranging them under and around the tree, and fully assembling the drum set, she still could not fall asleep. Her mind was back and forth between the excitement of Christmas Eve that still gave her butterflies in her thirties to the anxious anticipation of how Roger would likely ruin her happy morning. She imagined that he would either sit and watch in silence, maybe playing a game or two on his phone or frequently and vocally sighing from boredom and the fact that no matter what gifts she bought them, they were always wrong. The fact that she considered the former to be the best situation she could hope for was sad.

After hours of staring at the ceiling and trying not to move so Roger wouldn't yell at her for waking him up, she finally rolled out of bed and walked back out to the living room. She clicked on the Christmas Tree lights and sat in the beauty of the festive environment that she created. She leaned back on the couch and stared at the tree and the gifts until she drifted off to sleep.

Samantha awoke to the sounds of the kids running down the upstairs hallway to the stairs. She had no idea what time it was. It was still dark outside, but it looked as if dawn was approaching, and she could hear the morning birds start to sing. She jumped up and ran into the bedroom to get Roger.

"Merry Christmas," she said while gently rubbing his back. "The kids are getting up."

Roger grunted and rolled away from her.

It was hard for someone like her, who looked forward to this morning all year, to imagine just rolling over and not caring if the excitement of the morning was missed.

"Can you wake up? You don't want to miss the kids coming down, do you?"

He grunted again, but it sounded more like a defeated agreement.

Samantha ran back out of their room into the living room just as the kids ran down the stairs, their eyes barely open but their smiles ear-to-ear.

"Merry Christmas!" Samantha said to them and gave each of them a huge hug.

Sarah grabbed her stocking while Junior immediately ran to the drum kit and started banging away.

"Let's wait to open anything until Dad comes out, okay?"

Less than a minute later, Roger walked around the corner, saying, "What are you guys waiting for? Let's open some presents!"

As the kids excitedly tore into their gifts, Samantha sat down on the couch next to Roger. Just as her butt touched the cushions, he said, "Go grab a garbage bag, so this place doesn't turn into a mess."

Samantha stood and walked into the kitchen, grabbed a couple of garbage bags, brought them into the other room, stuffed some of the already ripped paper into the bag, and sat back down next to Roger.

"Mom, I can't get this open," Sarah said as she was trying to pull a doll out of the box.

"Go grab some scissors," Roger instructed Samantha.

She stood up again and walked into the kitchen to grab the scissors.

After helping Sarah cut the zip ties tightly, strangling the cute baby doll, she sat back down next to Roger again.

"Why don't you grab me a coffee while you are up?" Roger asked without even acknowledging that she had just sat down again.

Samantha walked back into the kitchen, still excited from her kids' happy faces, but her eyes welling up with tears as she felt more like an assistant to Roger than a wife and mother to his children. Who was she kidding? She was certain that he treated his assistant, Alice, better than that. She is like a favorite aunt that tells him like it is but takes care of him just the same.

She threw the breakfast casserole she prepared yesterday into the oven and brought the coffee out to Roger.

Samantha had just missed Sarah opening the Teacher Set she had been asking for. The set came with a stand-up whiteboard, folders, pens, crayons, markers, stencils, folders, bookmarks, grade books, and more. She was so in love with her teacher that she wanted to be just like her when she grew up.

Samantha handed the coffee to Roger, and he said, "Teacher Stuff? Really?"

"It was all she really asked for. It looks like she loves it already."

"Way to aim high, mom," he said sarcastically. "I would have bought her a doctor's kit so she can at least dream of a respected and paid profession when she grows up."

He looked down at his coffee, then to Samantha, who was not holding one, then sat his mug down on the coffee table.

"What's wrong with your coffee?" she asked.

"I just think it's odd that you made me one but didn't make yourself one. It's suspicious."

"I don't really want a coffee right now, but I can make one if it makes you feel better."

"Too late. Now I don't want it," he said as he pulled out his phone and started to play a game.

Chapter Forty-One

The New Year came and went, and Samantha reflected that she never quite got back to what she thought of as her 'pre-baby' self, but she didn't get worse until recently. This highly medicated, numbed-out, uninspired personality had become the new normal. But, since the trivia night out with Charlotte and friends last fall, she was downward spiraling into a deeper depression more than ever before. She was turning into what Roger always thought she was, to begin with. After getting her kids to school, she would watch movies and eat snacks on the couch. One day she really wanted an ice cream cake, so she went to the grocery store right down the street. On her way to browse the cakes, she ran into an old neighbor. After chatting for a few minutes, she walked back out of the store, horrified at the thought that someone would see her buy a cake for herself. She didn't go home, though. She drove for an hour to another town to another grocery store where she could buy the cake without witnesses. When she arrived home, she cut the cake into four pieces, put three pieces in three separate plastic containers then straight into the freezer. She put the other piece on a plate and sat on the couch while savoring the cool, creamy goodness. Halfway through the movie, she got up to use the bathroom and stopped by the freezer on the way back to the couch to grab another piece. When the movie was over, and she realized she had eaten half of an ice cream cake all by herself and with absolutely no exercise, she was disgusted. As she had a little pity party for herself, she started to worry about what would happen if Roger somehow saw the other two slices of cake or the box in the garbage. She jumped off the couch and ran to the freezer, where she frantically buried the two slices under the prepared meals that were already in there so they would not be visible. Then she grabbed the cake box out of the garbage, jumped in her car, and drove to the nearest gas station to throw it in the trash can between the pumps.

It was not a surprise that Samantha's clothes didn't fit. This only made matters worse. Not being able to fit in one of her cute outfits was a shot to her self-confidence; somehow, it made her even less driven, made her try less and less to look nice. She couldn't wear those cute shorts with that halter top Roger loves, so she threw on leggings and a big baggy sweatshirt of Roger's from college. She stopped curling her hair or even brushing it. She would just put it up on top of her head in a messy bun. It was the style anyway, right? She had not opened her make-up drawer for weeks and her jewelry sat unused, gathering dust.

When the kids would get home from school, she would try to put on a happy face, get them a snack, and help with homework. The two were very disciplined. They always did their work before going out to play with friends. She may not have control over herself, but her kids have turned out really great. They are perfect little angels all day. But there is the rare argument that oddly only happens when Roger is home.

Roger will come home and sit on the couch, watching the news. Yells can be heard from upstairs. It's likely just an insignificant fight over the remote control or about some obscure fact one of them happens to know that the other one doesn't.

"What the heck, Samantha? Is this how you control your kids? Do they fight all day like this? Take some control, would you?"

Tuesday:
I think I may call the school and let them know I cannot volunteer anymore. I don't have any clothes that fit AND are allowed per the dress code. I am not feeling like a very good role model, and I am getting worse and worse at faking it. It used to be when I had bad days or deeper depression, it would be obvious to my family, but I could pretend I was totally happy with the perfect life for others. This seems to be a skill I am losing.

I was invited to a baby shower and declined with a pretty weak excuse because I didn't want them to all talk about how much weight I had gained. A couple of moms from school invited me to have a drink one night, but there was no way I would eat in front of them; plus, what would I wear? When people see overweight women eat, they wonder why they are not eating a salad, and if they are eating a salad, why are they eating at all. I don't feel like being judged.

I wonder if the kids I read with at school would care if I wasn't following the dress code. I could just meet with the one sweet boy and help him. He needs the most help out of the four of them, and I don't want to let him down. Would he be angry if I showed up in athletic shorts and a hoodie? What would that judgmental receptionist say to me if I walked in wearing leggings, a baggy tee, and flip flops? I bet she would love to go all power-trippy on me and cite the Parent Volunteer Manual. Would she tell me I had to leave? What if I told her I didn't have any clothes that fit? Would she feel bad for me then point me towards the door or let it slide, since morbid obesity is a medical condition? I wonder if my reading group would notice that I gained weight. Kids say things without thinking. What if they commented on it? What if they were reading a passage about a hippo that couldn't stop eating, and they looked up at me? Am I strong enough to take that kind of criticism from an innocent child? Should I come up with an excuse as to why I gained weight, or should I be honest and let them know that it is not healthy to eat an entire ice cream cake in one sitting and what they are looking at is the consequence of doing so. I guess I could offer suggestions to them... maybe don't have two bowls of cereal.... stay away from pressurized cheese in a can. Would I cry if they said something? I have no idea what those kids deal with at home. Am I selfish to assume my weight gain would be a big event in their world? Is it nothing compared to what kids are going through? If I saw another volunteer, would I cry if they called me out about the dress code? I know I should just run to the store and pick up some clothes in larger sizes, but what if I try them on and they don't fit either? How many trips back and forth from the clothing racks to the dressing rooms do I have in me? I think I should call the school and cancel, then order every size online and just return what doesn't fit.... whatever keeps me from public meltdowns...

Chapter Forty-Two

<u>Thursday:</u>

I have not left the house in weeks.

Most days, I climb back in bed after watching the kids head out to school.

I told the volunteer coordinator that I needed some weeks off for personal reasons.

Strangers never ask about personal reasons, but they always assume the worst.

I haven't eaten much since I sleep all the time, but I have gained five pounds. I guess my metabolism shut down to keep myself from going into starvation mode since I'm not moving. My brain probably thinks I am dying.

Did Charlotte say she lost ten pounds after being sick just a few days or a week? Really? I don't think I could drop ten pounds in a month unless I lost a limb.

She keeps asking me to meet her for coffee or go for a walk or head out for dinner, but I just don't feel up to it. Coffee may be easy enough since I can go right after the kids leave for school. But, a walk... for exercise, no thanks, and dinner? No way I can't stay up late enough. Our dinners are getting *earlier and earlier, so I can just go to bed. I try to get to sleep before Roger gets home, so we don't have to engage. He still leaves his passive-aggressive notes on my grocery lists, and his sighs and mutterings have been louder and more frequent.*

The kids have been great about getting themselves to bed... I think. Well, I am not really sure because I am usually asleep. How much sleep is too much sleep, anyway? Don't they say sleep is important? Who is 'they'?

I wonder if they replaced me with a new volunteer at school. I wonder if my reading group feels abandoned by me or if they like having a new person better.

Why was Mr. Small so mean to me? What did I do to get on his bad side? Am I not pretty enough for him to be nice to me? He was so nice to Charlotte and actually treated her with respect. Surely, it can't just be because she is a volunteer... I'm a volunteer.... or I was. Most people are even nicer to strangers. That is why loved ones see our worst side.

I guess I will meet Charlotte for coffee. I just hope she doesn't tell me how she won the lottery or that one of her kids was picked to represent the state in an awesomeness contest or any of those things that, of course, would just fall in her lap.

Chapter Forty-Three

Samantha received an email from Junior's teacher to check in on her since she had no longer been coming into school to volunteer. She added that if Samantha would prefer some at-home volunteering, she really needed a parent to run to the library to pick up some books on hold for the class.

Samantha promptly wrote back, letting her know that she was fine, just working through some things, and she would be happy to pick up the books and send them to school with Junior the following day.

She headed to the library in a baggy sweatshirt (with no bra), a pair of leggings, and flip flops (even though it was still winter). She had not been to this library before and was amazed at how bright and cheery it was. The circulation desk was very contemporary and open, the computer stations looked state-of-the-art rather than the old run-down ones at the library across town. Even the sky-lights brightened up the whole room, making it unnecessary to even use lights or lamps.

She wandered around looking for the section where pulled, on-hold books were kept and noticed how peaceful it was in there. There were only a handful of elderly ladies in the whole place. She assumed most everyone else was at work or school, but who was she to judge other people for not utilizing this amazing resource when this was the first time she walked through these doors? She located the twenty or so reserved books for the class then walked them up to the circulation desk, which now had a fairly long line. It seemed as if the sweet group of old ladies was all ready to check out simultaneously. She decided to take a few minutes and check out their computers. She placed the books next to her and opened a browser. What would she search for on a public computer that was completely anonymous? The first thing she typed in the search bar was DEPRESSION. The results were too overwhelming to sort through, so she searched again, this time for EMOTIONAL ABUSE. She kept looking over her shoulder like she was afraid someone was watching what she was doing and even searched the ceiling for video cameras. She quickly changed the search phrase to DIVORCE. She found a few local divorce lawyer websites and clicked around. They try to make it sound so easy. Stuck in an unhappy marriage, just get divorced! As if it is that easy... no information about how much it costs, how possessions are split, how custody of the kids gets awarded, how evil people can find ways to manipulate the system and make one person look bad for no good reason and turn everyone they love against them, make them lose their children and leave them with absolutely nothing. She shuddered and changed the search phrase again, this time to ARSENIC POISONING. Before the results were displayed on the screen, she cleared the search bar, deleted the search history, closed the browser, and carried her books up to the now-empty line to check out her pile of books.

When Samantha arrived back home from the library, she found a beautiful flower arrangement on the front porch. She smelled the fragrant lilies and opened the card.

Happy Valentine's Day
Love, Roger

Samantha hurried inside to put the books down and dig out her phone, completely forgetting her very recent search history.

Chapter Forty-Four

Roger exited the conference room, exhaling rather loudly as he went, thinking how glad he was to have that meeting over with. Some meetings could actually be avoided if people used some sense. They just had a meeting to schedule a meeting. No agenda, no action items, no decisions... one hour of Roger's life he would never get back.

As Roger walked by the desks of some of the young admins, he glanced up.

"Hello, Mr. Sullivan." they each said in their best Marlyn Monroe 'Happy Birthday Mr. President' voice.

"Hi, ladies," he said with a half-smile. He heard the women giggle as he closed the door to his office.

His large table in the corner of his office was laid out with an amazing lunch spread. If there was one person he could count on, it was Alice. She knew exactly what to do and when to do it, without ever needing to be asked.

Alice was a seventy-year-old, petite, grandmother of nine with white hair. Most importantly, Alice is a highly qualified executive assistant. Most of the other executives had twenty-year-old ex-strippers as their assistants, but they were really not hired for their work quality. He actually needed an assistant, and Alice managed everything from his schedule and documentation to planning.

He sat down, ready to sink his teeth into an amazingly fresh-looking French Dip sandwich when Alice chimed in through the intercom.

"Mr. Sullivan, your wife, on line one."

He stood up, frustrated at having his lunch interrupted, walked over to his desk, and picked up the phone.

"What the heck, Samantha? Is something wrong? Why are you calling me at work?"

"Well, happy Valentine's Day to you too," Samantha said with a giggle.

"Hold on a second." Roger said as he put her on hold so he could intercom out to Alice's desk, "Alice, did you get anything for Samantha for Valentine's Day?"

"Roger," Samantha said with an icy, venomous voice. "It's still me."

Roger wasn't sure what to say, so he said nothing.

"I just wanted to call to thank you for the beautiful flowers, but I guess I should call Alice," Samantha said as she hung up the phone.

Roger stood at his desk, still holding the receiver in his hand, and yelled out to Alice to come into his office.

"Why didn't you tell me it was Valentine's Day? Why didn't you at least give me a heads up that you sent flowers to my wife?"

"I did, Mr. Sullivan. I told you both of those things multiple times, actually." She turned around, walked out, and closed the door behind her.

Roger couldn't help but chuckle at her boldness. There is not another woman in the world who could talk to him that way. He gently hung up the phone and went back to enjoying his lunch, now understanding the little heart Samantha had drawn on his coffee earlier that morning.

Chapter Forty-Five

Samantha met Charlotte at the quaint little coffee house down the street from their neighborhood. It sat right between the bar where they went to trivia night and an adorable gifts boutique. Samantha arrived first, ordered a Mocha for herself and a green tea for Charlotte, and found a nice table in the corner. She had butterflies. She had not seen Charlotte for a while. Last night she held such jealousy and animosity towards her, but sitting in the coffee shop, waiting for her, she was reminded that being with Charlotte put her at ease and made her a better person. She was so supportive, positive, kind, and giving. Samantha had not had a friend like her since high school. Charlotte's car pulled into the parking lot. She glamorously got out of her car, slowly opened the door to the cafe as the breeze fluffed her hair like she was in a shampoo commercial. A huge smile appeared on Charlotte's face when she made eye contact and ran over to greet Samantha with a hug.

"Oh my gosh, you didn't have to get my tea! Thank you, sweet friend!"

"I was here a bit early, so I thought I should go ahead and get us settled. Plus, I am happy to do it." Samantha said with a smile.

"So, how has your week been?" Charlotte asked while taking a sip of her tea.

"Well, I ate a whole ice cream cake, all by myself, alone, in my house, in two days," Samantha admitted. She couldn't believe she actually divulged something so personal and embarrassing to someone or something other than her journal.

"Wow, that sounds awesome!" Charlotte replied without the slightest hint of judgment.

"This is the first time I've left the house for anything other than chores since we went out to trivia night." The flood gates opened as Samantha prepared to bare her soul right there, in front of Charlotte, strangers, baristas, and all.

"Oh no, have you not been well?" Charlotte started to ask when Samantha dove in headfirst.

"Well, as it turns out, I have no self-discipline. I may plan to go out for a run and eat a tuna and cucumber sandwich for lunch, but instead, I walk my kids to school, then park my fat ass on the couch and watch movies and eat snacks until the kids come home."

"Oh, well..." Charlotte said with a bit more concern in her voice.

"I don't discipline my kids, and apparently, they are argumentative little devils. Plus, I'm a horrible wife and roommate."

"Wait right there." Charlotte tried to get a word in. "Your kids are sweet angels. They have the best manners, they do very well in school, and they are well rounded. Why are they, argumentative little devils?"

"They only seem to fight when Roger is home, and he says I have no control over the kids or our household. Maybe we should've gotten a nanny when they were small. Maybe I just wasn't up to being a mom. Maybe I am unfit to be a mom since I take medication for depression and anxiety…"

"Woah. That is bullshit. You are an amazing mom! Don't let anyone tell you otherwise. And what is this about being a horrible wife and roommate?"

The words poured out like they have been waiting for years, just beating on the back of the dam until now, when it finally broke. "I haven't been getting up early enough to get dolled up before Roger leaves, nor have I had his coffee and smoothie breakfast ready for him every morning like I used to. He thinks I am super lazy since I lay around all day, go to bed around eight, and sometimes sleep through when he leaves for work. I hear him sigh as he walks past the bed in the morning. He is simply disgusted by me. I have gained weight. I have no clothes that fit. He wants to have sex but has to wake me up when he comes to bed since I go to sleep so early. When he does, I am pretty sure I am just an object. I know he is thinking about someone else."

"How do you know that he is thinking about someone else? That is really assuming a lot, don't you think?"

"He tells me. He actually tells me that he is thinking about other women." Samantha finally paused.

Charlotte is a sweet, kind woman who always has a smile on her face. But Samantha noticed her soft, olive skin turn red, her eyes bulged out in quite a non-attractive way, and she was grinding her teeth.

"That asshole!" She yelled so loud that everyone in the coffee shop turned to see what was going on, but she continued, "How dare he treat you like that. How long has this been happening? Has he always been this way? You deserve better than to be treated like that." her voice was still very loud.

Samantha tried to take the conversation back to their private table, looked at Charlotte calmly, and waited for the other conversation in the room to start back up again. "It's always been this way. I guess it has just been getting harder over time."

Charlotte stared at Samantha and said in a much quieter but somewhat scarier voice, "Okay, let me give you a few facts…. Number one… I would never rush to get dressed just to make my husband coffee and see him off, and more importantly, he would never expect it. Two….. You cook amazing dinners every night, and he seems to think that is the norm. Does he have any idea how many of us order out at least half the week? Three… You are an amazing mom. Most moms just click around on their phones while their kids play or do homework. You are the most involved and loving mom, I know. And four….If a man ever told me he was thinking of another woman in bed… I would cut his dick off…. or at least leave the bastard and take everything he has."

Charlotte sat back, looking satisfied, and said in a coy voice with a small half-smile, "You know what you have to do, right?"

"I don't think I can cut his dick off. I probably wouldn't be able to commit, then it would just be a half dick and… well… maybe that's even worse." she trailed off.

"No!" she said as she leaned back into the table to get close like she was going to tell a secret. "You have to go home and talk to him. He needs to understand what the real world is like. This isn't the fifties, and actually, I'm damn sure those women in the fifties were not nearly as obedient as the history books say."

"I know you are right. I just am such a coward. What if he gets mad?"

"Just think of it as you giving him a chance to understand. You are taking the high road by helping him to see what marriage and parenting are really like. You're doing him a favor." Charlotte said.

Samantha was motivated to move forward with what she needed to do, but something was conniving in the look on Charlotte's face while she sat there rubbing her hands together like "Mr. Burns" from the Simpsons as if concocting an evil plan. Maniacal.

Chapter Forty-Six

Roger looked confused when he walked into the house. Samantha was standing in the kitchen in a cute outfit (possibly the last one that fit), with her hair curled nicely and her makeup finally liberated from the drawer and onto her primed face. She even had a few spritzes of perfume and simple yet classic earrings.

"What is going on?" he said, looking alarmed.

"I'm just glad you are home. Since it is Friday, both kids headed over to friends' houses for sleepovers. I was hoping we could have a nice dinner together and talk about some things."

"Some things? What could you possibly need to talk about?" he spat.

"How are things going at work? You never tell me about your job." she prompted.

"My job?" he laughed. "Do you really think you would understand my job? I bet you don't even remember what it is like to work, and you know nothing about IT."

"Okay, well, can we talk for a bit about us?"

"Us? What the heck, Samantha? What is going on with you?"

Well, I had coffee with Charlotte today. My eyes have been opened." she started as he looked at his phone distractedly. "Most moms, wives, or whatever, don't cook every single night of the week. Most of them go out every once in a while or even order in."

"What?" he laughed again. "You don't have enough time in your exhausting day to go to the store or to prep a meal. Oh, I am sorry. I didn't realize you were overworked" he rolled his eyes and looked back at his phone.

"A lot of husbands do chores to help around the house." Samantha started. "For example, Carrie Anne's husband walks their dogs, and Prescott does laundry for the whole family several nights a week."

He glared at her. He couldn't believe she was comparing him to that asshole, Prescott. That guy has it made with that hot wife and his 'dinner meetings.'

"I don't like the way you are treating me," she said, way louder than intended.

"Oh, really. You don't like living in a nice house, in a nice neighborhood, with a highly respected executive that women all want a piece of? You don't have to work, you have no responsibilities. You don't like the life I have given to you?"

"No, I really love my life, but I think you should be a little nicer to me. You never say thank you or..."

"Do you ever say thank you to me for working my ass off all week to provide for this family? "

She was starting to doubt herself. She no longer remembered what she was supposed to be arguing. She didn't know what to say anymore. Why didn't she write down some of the things that Charlotte said? She was so confident and sure of herself, which made Samantha feel that way too. But now she was unsure and had lost her way.

"So, are we done? Can I eat and watch the news, now?" he asked.

When she didn't answer right away, he grabbed his briefcase, walked off to the living room, and turned on the TV.

Samantha crept quietly into their room and went to bed at seven o'clock.

Chapter Forty-Seven

Samantha made sure to wake up early the next morning. It was Saturday, and she wanted to get dressed and get breakfast made. By the time Roger was up, she had a full breakfast prepared for him; scrambled eggs, bacon, toast with just a tiny amount of butter, a half grapefruit, coffee, and orange juice.

He walked in, sat down, and ate without saying a word. When he was finally finished, he walked past her on his way to the bedroom, saying, "I want you to end your friendship with Charlotte. You don't need friends like her. You don't need friends at all. You have us. You have me. I don't care what you tell her. Just break it off today."

Samantha found herself standing in the kitchen with his empty plate, bowl, glass, and mug in hand, simply stunned. Her chest was getting warm and tight. Her vision started to get dark around the edges. She dropped what she was holding into the sink and squatted down to the floor. Her heart was racing. Her breathing was getting quicker and more frantic. Her eyes were tearing up, and she felt she was going to break. She wanted to yell, she wanted to cry, she walked the tightrope between panic and frantic, leaning hard towards the latter.

She ran out of the door and towards Charlotte's house. She cried as she ran but still tried to get her breathing under control. Once she arrived, she knocked gently on the door. Prescott opened the door and immediately looked at her with pity. She wondered if Charlotte had told Prescott everything or if he just saw her tear streaks. Charlotte came out, put an arm over her shoulder, and walked her onto the porch closing the door between the two of them and Prescott, who remained inside.

"I did what you said." Samantha started.

"You cut his dick off?" joked Charlotte trying to lighten the mood.

"No!" she shouted. "I told him what you told me to. His expectations were too high. I'm a good mom and wife. I tried to stick up for myself."

"And...."

"He told me that we cannot be friends anymore," Samantha said under her breath.

"Ha!" Charlotte laughed out loud. But, seeing the look on Samantha's face, she stopped abruptly... "No, really?"

"Yes, so I came over to tell you that we can't see each other for a couple weeks."

"A couple weeks?" Charlotte was confused.

"Everything you said was right. I deserve better. I can pick my own friends. Don't worry. He cannot break up our friendship. I will take care of things." Samantha said as she started to calm down.

"What do you mean, "take care of things"? You are not talking divorce, are you? You guys are going to work this out, right?"

"Well, I cook all his meals and make him coffee every morning. He is too angry all of the time to notice if I were to slip something in," she said with a grin.

"You don't mean that Samantha, do you?" Charlotte said, looking at her sideways with the first judgmental look she had ever given.

"Oh, I'm just joking. Well, not about all of it. I do make his meals and coffee... and we can't be friends... but... well, just forget it. Can't you take a joke? I need to go." She ran off, and for the first time, she realized that she had never even put on her shoes when she left the house.

Samantha arrived home and walked back inside, with the face of someone truly broken and, not to mention, bloody feet. Roger was livid. "What the heck, Samantha? Is this how your friends treat you? I told you that you don't need friends. Friends are just trouble. Get a hold of yourself. Call your shrink. Take your meds. Do something to fix yourself, for crying out loud!" He stormed out of the house, jumped in his car, and sped out of the driveway.

Chapter Forty-Eight

Charlotte sat at her kitchen table, feeling sad and confused. She glanced out the kitchen window out to her backyard where Prescott was playing with the kids, but her mind was elsewhere. Roger seemed like such a nice guy, but he clearly treats Samantha horribly. Why would he not want her to be friends with his wife? They got along well the few times they were together. She didn't think he and Prescott hit it off, but she learned long ago that Prescott did not play well with other Alpha males. Samantha was hysterical. Could it be as bad as she says, or maybe her emotions just escalated the situation? Charlotte had not known Samantha for that long but couldn't imagine she would be capable of poisoning her husband if that is what she was implying.

She decided it would be best to reach out to Roger. He may be a jerk, but Samantha needed support and help. She thought about bouncing it off Prescott first, but nothing good would come of that. She had plans to run the kids to a birthday party within the hour. She would give Roger a call after lunch.

Chapter Forty-Nine

Roger drove aggressively down the road. He didn't know where he was going, but he knew he had to get away from Samantha and her never-ending drama. If it wasn't for him, they wouldn't have their nice house in their nice neighborhood. It would be fantastic if Samantha could just do anything. In the last couple of weeks, she has not only really let herself go, but she seems to not care that their house is a messy dump. She has been in bed most nights when he returns home, and he is the one who ends up having to help the kids with homework and make sure they are to bed on time. How can anyone sleep so much? Did she go to bed at 7pm and wake up at 7am? That can't be healthy.

He decided it would be a good idea for him to go for a run to burn off his anger, so he turned around and drove to the park by their house. It would be embarrassing if someone saw him drive the quarter-mile from his house to go for a run, but no one would have the balls to say anything to him anyway. He found a parking spot, grabbed his wireless headphones, and set out to run. He turned the volume up as loud as he could to drown out the thoughts in his head.

He ran around the campus trail three times and estimated his total run between four and five miles. He pushed himself harder than he had in a long time. He was exhausted when he sat back in his car. He wished that he had brought water, but chances were that they were out of them at home anyway.

Roger drove to grab a drink from the gas station near the back entrance of their neighborhood. He walked to the back cooler, grabbed a water bottle, and took it to the front for checkout. The little, old lady in front of him was slowly counting out pennies on the counter. He just wanted to throw his money at the attendant and leave, but he only had a twenty-dollar bill. He rolled his eyes and walked around the store to pass the time. When he was back up at the front, he saw that the lady was finally finished but that somehow three people had snuck in line since he left. He started getting himself worked up again. He threw the bottle into the candy rack and stormed back out to his car. He drove well over even the highway speed limit on their quaint, private neighborhood roads on his way home. But, then he saw Charlotte in her driveway.

Chapter Fifty

Home from the party and exhausted, the kids ran upstairs to relax in front of the TV. Charlotte walked out to the mailbox, wondering how she would get Roger's phone number without Samantha finding out. She absentmindedly stepped into the road and was almost plowed over by a car driving way too fast for a residential neighborhood. She turned to give the driver a dirty look. The car stopped, then backed up. She quickly turned and walked back towards her front porch without looking back, but she could hear the car aggressively pull into the driveway

"Charlotte!" She knew the voice before she even turned around. It was Roger, and he sounded angry. When she did turn, she saw that the look on his face was hateful, and he had a fire in his eyes. She had never been scared of another human being before, but she was now. He walked towards her slowly but with a sense of purpose. She was reminded of a zombie movie. They look through you with their dead eyes. They walked slowly towards you, but you somehow, no matter how fast you ran, you knew you wouldn't be able to escape.

Charlotte thought earlier about what she would say to him when she called, but suddenly seeing him in person, she lost her nerve.

"What the hell did you say to my wife?" he yelled.

Up close, she could see that his clothes were unkempt, his hair disheveled, and his face unshaven. He smelled of sweat and dirt. He looked like a caged animal that had finally managed to escape, and she was his captor. Charlotte tried to calm herself. Animals could smell fear. She quietly answered, "Samantha came over this morning. She was upset. I am really worried about her. Roger, I think you should..."

"You need to mind your own damn business. You don't get to tell me what I should or shouldn't do. You have been putting all of these crazy ideas in Samantha's head. What kind of friend does that? Everything was just fine until she started spending time with you."

She ignored the urge to wipe his spit from her face and saw that there was more collecting around his mouth. Was he foaming at the mouth? Was he rabid? "But, Roger, I think that..."

He interrupted again, "I really don't care what you think, truth be told."

They both turned around when they heard a second car pull in the driveway and roll to a stop beside Roger's car. Prescott hopped out of his car and looked back and forth between the two. "What the hell is going on here?" he asked specifically to Roger.

"You need to keep your wife in line." Roger spat.

Charlotte flinched as if she had been punched. First of all, she couldn't believe he would view a woman as someone who had to be 'kept in line' but also because she had never seen anyone talk to Prescott that way before. She watched as Prescott puffed out his chest and sized-up Roger, looking angrier than she had ever seen him. She was immediately afraid. Charlotte stepped in between the men to try to defuse the situation. "Roger, you need to leave."

But, before she had even finished her sentence, he turned, jogged back to his car, and peeled out, leaving skid marks on their driveway.

Chapter Fifty-One

Roger drove home, pulled into the driveway, and just sat in his car. Was Charlotte really that worried about Samantha? He didn't know what Samantha had told her, but he couldn't think of anything bad enough to be a cause for concern. She had become lazy, but as much as it got under his skin, it was not a big deal. He wondered if he had been going about this all wrong. Maybe, if he took on some of her duties over the weekend, she would rebound and be motivated to pull herself together.

He thought of pulling back out to pick up some flowers, but he didn't really want to go through the trouble. Plus, he didn't want her to think her behavior was okay. How could he be supportive without rewarding her for acting up?

As he expected, she was in bed when he arrived home, even though it was only mid-afternoon. She left a note saying she wasn't feeling well. He didn't know if that meant physically or mentally well, but either way, he was on his own for dinner. He grabbed the kids and took them out to their favorite restaurant. He would never admit to it, but it was a treat for him to go out with the kids, too.

Chapter Fifty-Two

The next morning, Samantha stayed in bed. She was so depressed, she couldn't move. Roger was in such a great mood, which was odd. He was so sweet and approached her, asking if she was feeling okay, did she need anything, don't worry about a thing, he will take care of the kids today.

Samantha just lay there. Not asleep, but hardly awake. Hours went by. She heard the kids laughing and playing with Roger. She began to doubt all the things she told Charlotte. Is he really just the great guy, hard-working husband, and caring father that everyone thinks he is, and somehow, she doesn't see it? Could she be the problem, not Roger?

Late afternoon, she could hear Roger get a phone call. She thought it was the right time to leave her room and try to be helpful. She took the kids outside to the driveway to give Roger some quiet time for his call. She backed Roger's car out to the end of the driveway and set up their portable pickleball net, which needed their garage and part of the driveway for setting up. She watched as the kids played, not quite feeling up to participating. As soon as Roger was off his call and came out, she told him she would make dinner and then go back to bed.

About an hour later, Samantha called the kids in from the driveway. She noticed Roger was on another call in the backyard, so she told the kids to wash up and wait to eat until their dad came back inside.

Minutes later, she was back in bed.

Chapter Fifty-Three

Roger could not believe the way the morning had started. He noticed there were no clean towels when he went to take a shower. "What the heck, Samantha?" he said in a quiet voice but loud enough that she would be able to hear if she was in the bedroom. He threw his towel from yesterday over the top of the shower and hopped in. After a few minutes of letting the glorious rain shower dump water all over his body, he grabbed for the shampoo. Empty. "What the heck, Samantha?" he said again, but even louder. He quickly finished his shower using a small sliver of soap, dried off with his day-old towel, and quickly got dressed.

He wasn't even surprised when he walked out of the bathroom, and Samantha was still sleeping. "I guess I will stop for coffee on the way to work today," he mumbled as he aggressively closed the door to the bedroom behind him. He heard the kids upstairs getting ready for school, and he supposed they would wake her up soon enough.

When Roger walked into the garage, convinced that he smelled like a moldy bath towel, he noticed his car was not in there. The garage door was open and the pickleball equipment was all over. As he saw his six-figure sedan sitting at the end of the driveway his moment of panic quickly got replaced by pure anger.

He walked out of the garage, stomping out to the car, noticing that it was not only sitting out in the open but also unlocked, with the key fob inside sitting on the dashboard.

He wanted to storm inside, wake that bitch up and make her get her act together. "What the heck, Samantha?" he said again at a yell once he got settled in his car. His car alerted him of an incoming call from the CEO, so he shoved down his anger and made a mental note to call her later on his long drive to work.

Thirty minutes later, as he pulled off the highway and made a turn towards a drive-thru coffee shop, he dialed Samantha's number. While the phone rang, he worked himself up all over again. She sounded asleep when she answered, which pissed him off even more.

"What the Heck, Samantha? You left the garage door open and, more importantly, my car unlocked with the keys in it at the end of the driveway all night. What is wrong with you?" Then he hung up.

Chapter Fifty-Four

Roger was fuming when he pulled into work forty minutes later. It was bad enough that his wife was a mess, but it took twenty-five minutes to get his order from the drive-thru for coffee.

"What the hell does she do all day that she can't take care of the basic needs of our family," he muttered to himself as he walked down the hall towards his office.

He normally enjoyed this time in the morning. He was able to park in his reserved parking spot in the underground garage right next to the executive elevator with a special key card that took him straight to the top floor. The employees who park out front in the large open-air parking lot and walk in the front doors past reception call the eighth floor the Ivory Tower. Every other floor is decorated in a nice, professional manner. However, the Ivory Tower has Travertine floors and walls as you exit the elevator, valuable, one-of-a-kind artwork, and high-end furniture in every executive's office.

It was nice for Roger to ride alone rather than have to smile at the lower level, kiss-ass employees who know him but whose names he will never know.

He sat in his office for a few hours, reviewing the reports he was planning to present to the board of directors later that day.

Alice knocked softly and asked if he would like a coffee. He accepted the offer for another coffee and got back to work.

A few minutes passed, and Alice walked briskly back in.

"Did you forget something, Alice?" he asked in a disrespectful tone noting her empty, coffeeless hand.

"I'm sorry, Mr. Sullivan, but there are some police officers on their way up to see you," she spoke rapidly, as if she may not get out all the words before he could see for himself.

In walked two uniformed officers with two men in cheap suits, which he guessed were plain clothes officers or detectives by the bulge at their hips. As Alice let herself out and closed the door, the tallest one spoke first. "Mr. Sullivan, Detectives Mann, and Esposito. We are investigating a murder that took place last night or early this morning, and we're following up on an anonymous tip we received."

He couldn't imagine what this had to do with him but knew the sooner he complied and helped, the sooner he could get his second cup of coffee and get on with his day. "Of course, detectives. What can I do to help?"

"Thank you for your cooperation, Mr. Sullivan. We would like to search your vehicle." said the shorter Esposito.

"My vehicle?" Roger said, half disbelieving and half sarcastic like he thought a coworker played a prank on him.

"Yes. We can do this now and get it over with, or we can come back this afternoon with a search warrant, more officers, and making a much bigger scene." Esposito stated again with the same unemotional tone.

Roger stood up and slowly walked between the four policemen, opened the door to his office, and motioned them to follow him. They walked past the three other offices between his own and the elevator. Thankfully, no other executives were in yet, but since every one of their admins was there, he had a feeling this situation would spread around the office very quickly. He began to walk faster in hopes of getting this cleared up, so he could yell at everyone to mind their own business and to get back to work.

The ride down to the underground executive parking garage was very uncomfortable and quiet, minus the instrumental version of The Girl from Ipanema playing softly in the background. When they exited the elevator, Detective Esposito asked Roger to stand over to the side with the two officers and point to his car. Roger walked over to the officers, looking very put out, clicking his key fob making his car just two parking spots away, beep and flash its headlights to unlock the doors. Esposito and Mann both nodded to the officers as if they were sending secret signals and walked over to the car.

While Detective Mann walked a lap around the car, Roger scoffed, clearly agitated, and rolled his eyes at the officers as if to say, "Detectives... am I right?"

Mann then opened the drivers' side front door and looked directly under the seat. Roger shifted his weight and crossed his arms like a pouting toddler. Just then, his arms fell to his side, and the angry, aggressive stance was replaced with a more defensive posture. Detective Mann was pulling a long chef's knife out from under the seat with his gloves and placing it into a plastic bag Esposito was holding open marked with large, red letters spelling EVIDENCE.

Chapter Fifty-Five

Samantha stepped out of the shower, still red-faced and sweating. She spent the entire morning cleaning the house from top to bottom to get her mind off the phone call she received from Roger.

Then, her phone rang. It made her flinch with worry that it was Roger to yell at her more, but one look at the caller id told her it was her mother.

"Hi, mom. I'm just getting out of the shower. Can I call you back later?"

"Sammy, I am so sorry. I am going to pick up your kids from school and take them to my house, okay." she was talking so fast, "Sam, do you even know what has happened?" her mom sounded hysterical. "Charlotte has been murdered. Turn on the news."

Without saying goodbye, Samantha put the phone down and walked over to the TV. The reporter from the local news station was standing outside Charlotte's house just around the corner from where she was standing. The title across the bottom of the screen said, "Local Mom found Murdered." Samantha turned around. Her chest was getting tight, her breaths were getting shorter and shorter. She stumbled into the bathroom to get her anti-anxiety/ panic attack pills. She tossed two down her throat and swallowed them dry. She tried to take deep breaths but started to get dizzy. She crawled into bed and thought about calling Roger. Just as she stared at the phone, thinking about making the call, it rang. The caller id was of no help in identifying the unknown number.

"Hello?" Samantha said in a soft, timid voice.

"Mrs. Sullivan, this is Detective Mann. We have your husband in custody, being held for questioning in the murder of Charlotte Callahan. We are almost to your house with a warrant to search the property and just wanted to give you a quick heads up. We will be there in two minutes." and he hung up.

Samantha was still holding the phone in a daze when the loud and forceful knocks rapped on the door. She threw on a pair of shorts and a hoodie and ran to answer the constant pounding.

When Samantha opened the door, a tall man in a suit held a detective badge in one hand and a piece of paper in the other, which she just assumed was the warrant. She stared at him and the items he held in his hands as a half dozen officers pushed past her into her home.

"Ma'am, this will go a lot faster if you can help us." said the shorter stocky man in a suit pulling up the rear. "Please point us to your computers and all electronic devices."

Samantha was in shock, but at least she was no longer hyperventilating. "The computers and devices currently home are all plugged in around the corner in the office. Look, I just took some heavy medication and need to lay down before I pass out. Please, do what you need to do and leave."

She dragged herself to her bedroom, feeling dizzy and loopy. She closed the door and flopped onto her bed, still fully dressed, on top of the covers.

Chapter Fifty-Six

Mann and Esposito rode together back to the station after searching the Sullivan home. They were both quiet most of the ride, trying to process everything they had learned.

"So," Mann started and broke the silence. "We went through his personal phone, his work phone, his work computer, their home computer, and two iPads, and what did we find?"

"Well, he may be a pompous asshole, but he seems to be a one-woman man. No signs of having an affair with anyone. Not Charlotte, no women from work, no women from his travel…." said Esposito trailing off as Mann's cell phone rang.

"Detective Mann." he answered, paused nearly thirty seconds then, "Thanks." and hung up.

"Location tracking has been accessed. The only two locations that his work cell phone and work computer have been to over the last two weeks have been his home and his office. The iPads and home computer have not left the house."

"And? But? I know you have something else. Don't tease me, Mann! Spit it out!"

"Over the last two weeks, his personal cell phone has been to the office, back home, and 320 Sycamore.... Charlottes house... just this past Saturday. So, now we have the weapon, and we can place him at the scene."

The men shifted back to silent mode as they parked and walked into the station. An officer up front let them know that Roger was in holding while he waited for his lawyer to arrive and that the victim's husband was picked up for questioning and was waiting for them in Interview Room 3.

Chapter Fifty-Seven

Detective Esposito made his way into Interview Room 3 to talk with Mr. Callahan. At the same time, Mann updated their files with the information they had received from the forensic technicians and everything they learned from their searches.

Esposito thought he knew what he was in for as he frequently ate dinner with his wife at the same restaurant that Prescott Callahan frequented with his co-workers. The detective recognized him right away but was surprised at his demeanor. When he saw him out, Prescott was very bold, loud, and flirty. He seemed to have a new, long, amazing story to tell each time he saw their group. The other people at the table would hang on to his every word, then they would ooh, ahh, and laugh at all the right places. He was a performer and his co-workers, his audience. But today, the man that sat in front of him was far from Mr. Popularity. He was not sobbing but had a look on his face that said that he would be if his tears had not all dried up. His eyes were swollen and red, his hair was a mess, and the detective assumed he was still wearing the same clothes he must have been wearing last night by the wrinkles.

"Mr. Callahan. I am Detective Esposito. I am terribly sorry for your loss."

The broken man just looked through him like he wasn't there.

"I would like to ask you some questions about your wife's relationship with Roger Sullivan."

"Roger?" Prescott said as he finally made eye contact. "What about him?"

"What was your wife's relationship with Mr. Sullivan?"

"She tolerated him more than I did. He's an asshole. But Charlotte is nice to everyone... was nice to everyone." he corrected.

"Are you aware that he was at your house Saturday?"

"Yes. I'm aware." Prescott stated defensively as if Esposito was trying to tell him something about his wife that he was unaware of.

"Do you know why?"

"Charlotte met with Roger's wife, Samantha, on Friday morning for coffee. Charlotte was upset Friday. She told me about how Roger was an even bigger jerk than she thought. She was sure that Samantha was emotionally abused and that she deserved better. I asked her for details, and she clammed up. She didn't like sharing her friend's personal information that she was entrusted with." Prescott looked even sadder as he remembered his last days with his wife.

He cleared his throat, tried to compose himself, and continued, "The next morning, Samantha showed up at our door. Not only did she look as if she had been crying, but Charlotte was even more upset when Samantha finally left. Again, she wouldn't tell me anything. I was on my way out to go to the gym and catch the second half of the early football game with some friends. She said we would talk about it later and that I would be late for my trainer if we got into it then. So, I left. Maybe I shouldn't have, but I left."

Prescott paused, but Esposito knew better than to chime in. If they are talking, let them keep talking. He wasn't done yet, and the detective knew it.

"When I pulled in the driveway that afternoon, Roger was there. It was strange enough for him to be there without Samantha, but it just got weirder. When I got out of the car, I could see that he was arguing with my wife. He was yelling at Charlotte. She was angrier than I have ever seen her, but she also looked scared. Her face was red, and she may have been crying. She said something about how she was worried about Samantha, but Roger kept repeating over and over that it was none of her business. They both seemed shocked when I walked up. Roger took one look at me and stormed off to his car and drove off towards his house." he paused, took a deep breath, then continued.

"When we walked inside, Charlotte was immediately greeted by our kids who...." The mention of his kids made him flinch. "Oh my God, what are the kids going to do?"

Esposito handed him a tissue and gave him a minute to recompose himself.

"The kids must've heard the argument, so they were downstairs waiting for us to walk in. They thought it was the two of us fighting. She walked them upstairs with a smile, letting them know everything was okay. She fell asleep with them after getting them to bed. The next morning, I had hoped to talk to her in private about everything that happened, but she made breakfast like her normal happy self as if nothing happened. The day was pretty busy, and it never came up again, so I left it alone."

Finally, Detective Esposito was ready to drop the bomb. He wanted to see Prescott's reaction. He had hoped Mann would be back in the interview room by now, but he couldn't wait. "Are you aware that we found a knife, very much like the one that was used to kill Charlotte, under the front seat of Roger Sullivan's car?"

Prescott went from confused, to shocked, to intense anger in five seconds. He jumped up and threw his chair into the wall. Two officers ran into the room, but Esposito politely asked them to leave. Prescott stopped throwing things but continued to pace the room. He looked like a caged lion who was teased with a taste of fresh meat.

The detective's cell phone vibrated, indicating an incoming text message.

RS attny otw. heading to room 2.

Prescott was not in a state to leave, and thankfully, he couldn't see out of the window anyway. Esposito decided to let him settle down a bit and wait for Roger and his lawyer to get situated in the next room.

Prescott stood still and stared at the wall for a while, then snapped out of his trance, saying, "I need to get home to my kids. Can I go home and come back tomorrow if you still have more questions?" He looked sad but in control. His priorities seemed to have changed from revenge to caring for his children.

Detective Esposito nodded, and they walked towards the door. He peered out into the hall and noticed the door to the room next to them was closed, and therefore, most likely occupied. The two walked out: the detective and a sad, broken man who just became a single father.

Chapter Fifty-Eight

Apparently, Roger's attorney had arrived. He was the kind of person that everyone knew was around. He walked in wearing what looked to be a very expensive suit, very metrosexual style with trendy hair and constant duckface as if he were trying to impress the cameras. He talked at an elevated volume to let everyone know he would not leave without making a huge scene, directing everyone to move Roger out of holding and get him in a private room where they can talk. "No cameras, no two-way mirror observers, no audio recordings. Total privacy. Please tell me you have a decent coffee machine around here." He made himself at home, taking whatever he needed or wanted, and waited to be directed to his client.

Mann was on his way to grab Esposito from the interview room with Prescott, but the two were already walking out of the room by the time he got there. The whole station seemed to be more chaotic than normal. They both eyed each other like two prison guards on Friday the 13th and a full moon. The air was thick with tension.

Prescott was right behind Esposito; he looked like a beaten man, lost and despondent. Mann walked up next to Esposito and leaned over to let him know, privately, that an officer would be escorting Roger down to the interview room next door to talk to his attorney.

Suddenly Prescott moved like a big cat pouncing on a gazelle. When the detectives turned around to see what was happening, they saw Prescott dive on top of Roger, whom they hadn't seen walk up behind them, and wrestle him to the ground.

"Why couldn't you just stick to abusing your own wife?" Prescott screamed, and spittle flew from his lips.

The commotion all came to a sudden stop when Prescott realized that Roger was not fighting back. He looked down at him through wild and teary eyes. Was he knocked out? Prescott jumped up and backed away, staring at the body on the floor, simply horrified.

Mann knelt down next to Roger to see where he had hit his head and if he had been knocked out. Esposito immediately grabbed Prescott and called on his walkie for a 10-53 outside the interrogation rooms. Mann checked the pulse the looked up at Esposito with a shake of the head. "Make that a 10-54. He's dead."

Prescott began crying hysterically and screaming absolute nonsense. Mann stayed with the body while Esposito walked Prescott off to holding, so they could get the ambulance, coroner, and medical examiner in as soon as possible.

Epilogue

<u>Monday:</u>

I took a walk today and began to think of what my life would be like without Roger. I don't even remember how to be my own person. I feel that I am always trying to conform to what he wants me to be rather than who I am. In my perfect world, I would still have my kids and my house and all the money we need and live just like we do now 80% of the time when Roger is not home. I already know how to be a single mom, so the only difference would be the lack of stress of living up to Roger's grand expectations. But this isn't a perfect world. If I chose to leave Roger, I would have no money. I have not worked since Junior was born and don't even know what I am qualified for anymore. Nothing would be worse than losing my kids.

What if he tries to take the kids from me? What if he tells the courts that I am unfit and lets them know all about my depression and anxiety? He has been the only one to see me at my worst when I am falling down the bottomless pit of a panic attack. Will he turn against me, take my kids, and leave me with nothing? I can handle his constant, unrealistic pressure for the rest of my life if it means keeping my kids. I can never let him take my kids. I love my kids. I don't think I could live without my kids. I started to hyperventilate on my walk and fell to the ground on a curb in our neighborhood. I started crying hysterically. I couldn't stand, I couldn't breathe, I couldn't do anything but think that I could never lose my kids. When I was finally able to stand and walk the rest of the way home, I thought it odd that no one stopped to check on me. Is it normal to drive by a woman crying on the side of the road, or is it just that no one cares?

People always say they will be there for you, but no one means it. They will only do what is in their best interest. I am completely and totally alone.

Tuesday:

Roger was so angry this morning. We had a power outage last night, so I woke late and had to give him his lunch, coffee, and breakfast in my pajamas. He reminded me that there were still items on my list he gave me, like ...

- cleaning out the kid's closets and taking old clothes to be donated
- organize the playroom closet
- send a birthday card to his aunt in Michigan

- call the school and demand that Junior get a second tryout for basketball since he was sick the second day of tryouts.
- be sure to get a good long workout in because 'my butt just isn't what it used to be.'

I think I will just go back to bed since I am still in my pajamas and take a little nap before I tackle the list.

Friday AM:

Charlotte and I met for coffee this morning.

When she arrived and asked how I was doing, I just burst out crying. Since I stopped seeing Dr. Pager, I have not had anyone to vent to privately. I have never really revealed anything to Charlotte about my marriage or my mental health before. Even when she says things like how she cannot believe Roger never goes to parties with me, I always pretend to not care. One thing being married to Roger has taught me is how to be a convincing actor. But, this morning, all of my frustrations and worries came out so fast I couldn't stop them. I told her how perfect he wants his home life to be. How even when he is wrong, I am the one who has to beg for forgiveness. I told her some of the hateful things he has said to me and how he thinks I am a bad wife and mother.

Friday PM:

I planned to talk to Roger. I planned to fix our marriage. I planned for us to start a brand new life tonight, then fall asleep in each other's arms. I spent the whole night alone, in tears, feeling broken. My chest hurt so bad, and my eyes were swollen. What have I done to deserve this pain?

Saturday AM:

I ran over to Charlotte's house. I explained to her that we couldn't be friends for a while. She asked why and I told her that Roger said we couldn't be friends anymore. She laughed. She actually laughed. Like she couldn't believe anyone could tell me what to do or not do. When she saw I was serious, she asked if that was true, then why would I not see her just for a while? I told her that I would take care of it. Surely there are several substances I could slip in his coffee. Then hopefully we could be friends again. She looked horrified. I laughed and laughed. It was more of a 'crazy, wide-eyed, out-of-control' laugh than an 'oh I'm just kidding' laugh, and she knew it. When I stopped laughing and wiped my teary eyes on my shirt, I ran. If I had stayed another minute, she would have told me I needed to 'see someone.' Ugh, how many times have people said that to me? There is no one to see that can help me. No one can fix me, not without talking about my childhood, forgotten tragedies, uncomfortable silence, or even medication. The first question they always ask is, "are you a threat to yourself or others?" uh, yeah, but I'm sane enough to not say that! I would never harm myself because I love my kids too much. But, I would do just about anything to protect them. I told Charlotte that she didn't know how to take a joke. She clearly didn't believe in me any more than Roger did, and maybe it is best that we cannot be friends anymore. My chest hurts, my heart hurts.

Saturday PM:

Roger has been gone all morning, and it is now after lunch, and he is still not home. I pull up Find My iPhone and wait for our devices to locate. I do this sometimes, hoping maybe I can catch him in an affair and have an easy reason for a clean divorce, but every time, he is just at the office. The locations of all devices seem to be here. How is that possible? Roger always takes his phone with him. I zoomed in on the location to see that, actually, all devices are in our neighborhood. Roger is at Charlotte's house. Why would he be there? That is not the affair I was hoping to catch him in. Then it hits me. I bet she called him. She must have called him to tell him what I said to her. How could she betray me? She hates Roger! I thought she was my friend. How could she do this to me?

I put a note on the kitchen counter saying that I am not feeling well and had to go to bed early. I also suggested that maybe Roger should sleep in the guest room, although chances are, he will sleep on the couch anyway.

<u>Sunday:</u>

I heard Roger let himself outside for a phone call. He sounded angry and was being quite vulgar. I am sure the kids heard, and they were not used to hearing that from him either. So, I took them out into the driveway. I pulled Roger's car out to the end of the driveway, so the kids had more room to play. I set up their pickleball set, then I remembered I wasn't supposed to be feeling well, so I went back inside, threw a frozen lasagna in the oven, and made a salad. When dinner was ready, I called everyone in and went back to bed. I must have fallen asleep again because I awoke to a conversation in the distance. Once I was fully awake and coherent, I realized it was Roger. He was in the kitchen talking with the kids over dinner. They talked about the game of pickleball, school, and friends. It sounded like a nice healthy conversation. I cannot lose my kids. I cannot lose my family.

<u>Sunday PM/ Monday Early Morning:</u>

I lay awake until I could tell everyone was asleep. The kids were quiet by 9pm, and Roger turned off the TV and fell asleep on the couch by eleven. Just after midnight, I got out of bed, slipped on my shoes, and opened my bedroom window. I pulled out my phone and sent a quick text to Charlotte telling her Roger was out of control, and I needed to come to see her, and that I wanted to apologize for everything I had said. As I suspected, she told me that Prescott was still out and probably would be for a while, so I should just come on over. I jumped out of the bedroom window, walked in the shadows in other people's yards until I reached Charlotte's house. She sat on the front porch waiting for me. I told her I was sorry, and she assumed it was for the argument we had. She turned towards to front door and reached out for the handle exposing her long, bare, beautiful neck. I pulled the knife that I had carefully hidden out of my back pocket, raised my arm, and quickly pulled it across the flawless, tight skin covering her throat. I turned to leave. I didn't look back as I heard her drop to the ground. I would miss her, but it was the right thing to do. She could not; she would not put me at risk of losing my kids. I walked quietly and calmly home, sticking to the shadows. When I get back to our house, I carefully placed the knife under the front seat of Roger's unlocked car still parked at the end of the driveway and climbed back through my window. I stripped naked, threw my clothes in a bag, stuffed it under my bed, took a sleeping pill, and went to sleep.

Monday AM:

I woke up very groggy and stumbled out to wave to the kids as they headed off to school. I went straight back to my bed and fell face-first into my pillow and back to sleep.

A couple minutes later, I woke again, with a start as my cell phone rang on my bedside table. My heart was racing as I tried to comprehend what was happening.

I looked at the caller ID and saw it was Roger. The first thing out of his mouth, "What the Heck, Samantha? You left the garage door open and, more importantly, my car, unlocked with the keys in it, at the end of the driveway, all night. What is wrong with you?" Then he hung up.

As I dialed the anonymous tip line for the local police, I grinned and giggled to myself.

To think he was mad about the car....

About the author

Cori Nevruz is originally from Raleigh, North Carolina, and now resides in Wilmington, North Carolina, with her husband and three sons. Cori is a graduate of the NCSU and works from home as a website designer. She has previously written several children's books that feature student illustration giving over 100 children published illustrator credit. She's also an active volunteer at her boy's schools, an avid reader, potty humor enthusiast, and a strong believer in the power of kindness.

About 5310 Publishing: Canadian-based, 5310 Publishing has operations worldwide, selling books in multiple countries and languages. Since 2018, 5310 has published adult, young adult books, and coloring books.

Follow us on Twitter and Instagram: @5310publishing
For more books, go to 5310publishing.com

If you enjoyed this book, please review it.

CPSIA information can be obtained
at www.ICGtesting.com
Printed in the USA
LVHW090556070721
691973LV00003B/138